COMING NEXT TIME...

**STORIES! ARTICLES!
SHERLOCK HOLMES & DR. WATSON!**

*Sherlock Holmes Mystery Magazine #27
is just a few months away...watch for it!*

I0547272

Not a subscriber yet?
Send $59.95 for 6 issues (postage paid in the U.S.) to:

**Wildside Press LLC
Attn: Subscription Dept.
7945 MacArthur Blvd, Suite 215
Cabin John, MD 20818**

You can also subscribe online at
www.wildsidepress.com

FROM WATSON'S NOTEBOOKS

My story about Sherlock Holmes and Wisteria Lodge appears in the current issue of *Sherlock Holmes Mystery Magazine* as well as Jack Grochot's translation of my notes concerning the Brixton Jewel Theft. I am also pleased to read a new piece by O'Neill Curatolo concerning quail and partridge. Peter James Quirk returns with an article about the Kray twins, as nasty a pair of villains as you'll find in London's history.

—John H Watson, M D

✗ ✗ ✗ ✗

New stories by "recidivists" include Peter James Quirk, Laird Long and Steve Shrott, whose protagonist takes a leaf from Pacino's book. T.J. Glenn, a regular *Weird Tales* author, regales us with a new case for Dr. Augustus Argent, and S. Subramanian pens about another missing case in "The Adventure of the Tired Captain."

Canonically Yours,
Marvin Kaye

✗

SHERLOCK HOLMES
MYSTERY MAGAZINE

VOL. 7, NO. 5   Issue #26

FEATURES

From Watson's Notebooks, *by John H Watson, M D* 4
Ask Mrs Hudson, *by (Mrs) Martha Hudson.*. 5

NON FICTION

Screen of the Crime, *by Kim Newman* 10
Quail, Partridge, Rubbish Bird, *by O'Neill Curatolo*. 15
The Kray Twins, *by Peter James Quirk* 18
The Whole Art of Detection: Book Review, *by Eugene D. Goodwin* 29

FICTION

The Adventure of the Tired Captain, *by S. Subramanian*. 30
What Would Pacino Do?, *by Steve Shrott* 45
The Occurrence of the Air Apparent, *by Teel James Glenn*. . . . 55
Retribution, *by Peter James Quirk* 63
Murder at a Military Funeral, *by Archie Goodwin* 76
Gutsy, *by Laird Long* 82
The Brixton Jewel Theft Caper, *by Jack Grochot*. 88
Above Suspicion, *by Victoria Weisfeld* 105

The Adventure of Wisteria Lodge, *by Sir Arthur Conan Doyle*. . .123

ART & CARTOONS

Elena Betti . . . . Front Cover
Marc Bilgrey 2

STAFF

Publisher: John Betancourt
Editor: Marvin Kaye
Non-fiction Editor: Carla Coupe
Assistant Editor: Steve Coupe

Sherlock Holmes Mystery Magazine is published by Wildside Press, LLC. Single copies: $10.00 + $3.00 postage. U.S. subscriptions: $59.95 (postage paid) for the next 6 issues in the U.S.A., from: Wildside Press LLC, Subscription Dept. 7945 MacArthur Blvd, Suite 215, Cabin John, MD 20818. International subscriptions: see our web site at www.wildsidepress.com. Available as an ebook through all major ebook etailers, or our web site, www.wildsidepress.com.

ASK MRS HUDSON

by (Mrs) Martha Hudson

My Dear Mrs Hudson,

My husband Ralph and I live in Hyannis, Massachusetts, in that part of America called New England. We have both read Washington Irving's sketches of things British and are eager to spend our coming vacation in London. We will appreciate any advice you have to give about places we ought to visit while in your great city and its environs. We are especially interested in Shakespeare and have read all of Charles Dickens's novels.

Gratefully,

Amanda Carpenter

✗   ✗   ✗

Dear Mrs Carpenter,

I am familiar with Washington Irving's articles about British locales and am sorry to tell you that some, as for instance the tavern supposedly frequented by Sir John Falstaff, are long gone. However, there are still ever so many places that I am certain will be worthwhile for you to see, and in this I would not rule out such popular tourist attractions as the changing of the guards at the Palace and of course you'll want to visit the Tower of London. You may also wish to go to Greenwich, which is a short bus ride away from the Tower; there you will see an old ship, the *Cutty Sark*, as well as one of the royal family's off-residencies and it is open to the public. In Greenwich there is a fascinating nautical museum, as well.

Do plan a day trip to Stratford, where you may indulge your interest in Shakespeare. As for Dickens, one of the houses he lived in on Doughty Street is now open to the public; it is not far from the British Museum. If you would like to see a genuine Dickens manuscript, the Victoria and Albert has *The Mystery of Edwin Drood* and if you go there you will be quite close to that amazing shopping centre, Harrods. It is in the section of London called Knightsbridge, which Gilbert referred to in a now-obscure joke in *The Mikado*. (A word of advice concerning the V & A—write to them well before you come to London and ask permission to see the Dickens manuscript.)

If you don't mind another day trip, visit Rochester, where Dickens lived as a child and returned to at the close of his life. I have been there and was delighted at the main street with its plaques pointing out scenes that were set in various Rochester places. If you are familiar with the Edwin Drood tale, the school where young Rosa Bud lived is now a Dickens museum; the original of the choirmaster's living quarters is there as well, as is the cathedral itself, though in the book, Rochester is renamed Cloisterham.

I asked Dr Watson for further suggestions and he says he would be delighted to show you about the city. I cannot imagine a more engaging host!

With warm regards,
Martha Hudson

✗ ✗ ✗ ✗

Dear Martha Hudson,

I wonder whether Mr Holmes is at all religious. Ditto yourself and Dr Watson.

Respectfully,
The Reverend Matthew Lloyd Kent

✗ ✗ ✗

Dear Reverend Kent,

I belong to the Church of England, which also is called the Anglican Church. Dr Watson is a member as well, though he seldom attends services. Mr Holmes, however, is not at all religious and if asked expresses views I am sure you would find distasteful. Yet, perhaps paradoxically, he has great respect for the clergy and as for religious principles, he has devoted his life to fighting evil.

Very Truly Yours,
Mrs Hudson

✗ ✗ ✗ ✗

Dear Mrs Hudson,

If it is not too intrusive, I wonder about your household budget and how you manage it.

An Inquiring Accountant

✗ ✗ ✗

My Dear Inquirer,

I do not mind discussing this with you, though I cannot presume to know much about budgeting other than the everyday necessity of running this household. My mother had a flair for this subject and did what she could to train me. I confess that I did not always pay as much attention as I ought, but I still ended up knowing a great deal about personal economy.

I keep two ledgers that I bought from a nearby stationer's shop. One is for income and the other covers expenses. The secret I have found is never miss a day, but enter all sums as soon as possible, keeping a running total of both income and costs by category. In this, I am fortunate for always liking mathematics. If I say so myself, I do have a head for figures.

Sincerely,

Mrs Hudson

✗ ✗ ✗ ✗

Dear Mrs Hudson,

Recently you dismissed a letter asking about your husband as something you do not wish to discuss. While one must respect your wishes, it does pique one's curiosity. Isn't there anything you could say about him?

Miss Donna Flynn

✗ ✗ ✗

Dear Miss Flynn,

I do understand your curiosity. I will tell you this much about him. He is a man whose choices ultimately led to his downfall. Mr Holmes was involved in that process, as were both Dr Watson and Inspector Lestrade. This is, as you must see, a painful thing for me, so please rest assured that it is a sad story at best.

Mrs Martha Hudson

✗ ✗ ✗ ✗

Dear Mrs Hudson,

I live about twenty miles northwest of London and have no access to one of your phone books so I cannot be in touch with Dr Watson. Thus I am writing you in hopes that you will pass this along to him.

I am thinking of writing a mystery novel and am therefore interested in effective methods of suicide.

Thank you for your assistance.

William Clyde of Elstree

✗   ✗   ✗

Dear Mr Clyde,

By the time you read this, you may have met Dr Watson as he spoke with medical authorities in your town in reference to your letter. When he read it, he feared you meant to kill yourself. That may seem to be an over-reaction, but physicians always treat questions and statements about suicide as potential cries for help.

I trust you are receiving caring treatment from the doctor.

Mrs Hudson

✗   ✗   ✗   ✗

This issue's recipe is one for shrimp with butter. When I was young, it was not easy to find fresh shrimp in London, but that is no longer the case. The below procedure is easy and tasty.

SHRIMP WITH BUTTER

1 pound of cooked shrimp
2 tablespoons of butter
2 egg yolks
½ cup of dry white wine
Nutmeg

1. Melt the butter and combine it with the wine.

2. Combine the butter/wine with the shrimp.

3. Place the mixture in a double boiler and heat for a short time.

4. Beat the egg yolks.

5. Make sure the flame is not too hot before pouring one table-spoon of it over the eggs.

6. Repeat step 5 until the yolks are thinner and not curdled.

7. Pour the eggs over the shrimp mix and stir until it thickens.

8. Remove the mixture from the heat and stir in grated nutmeg.

SCREEN OF THE CRIME

by Kim Newman

If you're trying to collect Sherlock Holmes films and TV on DVD, then you can now fill a couple of gaps by heading to Amazon.de (or any other Amazon platform) and ordering the German releases of *The Return of Sherlock Holmes* (1986)—*Eine Pfeife in Amerika*—and *Sherlock Homes Returns* (1993)—*Die Rückkehr des Sherlock Holmes*. For some reason these mostly American TV movies don't seem to have any official releases in the UK or the US. Both these Region 2 discs offer German-dubbed audio but also have the English soundtrack—without forced German subtitles (indeed, without the option for any subtitles). Extras are limited to a few trailers, and transfers are fair only—TV movies in the '80s and '90s seem pretty hideous now with their soft video blur look and bland set-ups. TV from the 1960s and '70s holds up much better on digital media than products from this era, when even prestige productions tended to look and sound cheap. Neither of these soundalike efforts are exactly top drawer—though *The Return of Sherlock Holmes* runs to location shoots in the UK, Boston, and Arizona and *Sherlock Homes Returns* (aka *1994 Baker Street*) gets around San Francisco fairly nippily.

Both films—like seemingly 75% of TV movies ever made—serve half-heartedly as pilots for series that never came along. Indeed, they seem very much like different takes on pilots for the same TV series, so watching them back to back is a bit like looking at "The Cage" and "Where No Man Has Gone Before," the variant pilots for *Star Trek* or *Wonder Woman* (1974) and *The New Original Wonder Woman* (1975), successive stabs at what became the 1970s *Wonder Woman* TV show. Both have Holmes go into cryo-suspension around the turn of the century—writing out the bee-keeping retirement and "His Last Bow"—and being defrosted in the present day (at time of recording) and teamed up with a female American Watson figure to go after the modern-day equivalents of the crooks he used to catch and establishing a contemporary version of his consulting detective practice. Both are in fact straight lifts from the BBC-TV series *Adam Adamant Lives!* (1966-67), in which a dashing Edwardian adventurer survives on ice into the 1960s and teams up with a dolly bird in *Avengers*-lite adventures. To be fair, the reawoken man out of time protagonist, whether a hero of old or a fish out of water, has been around since Rip Van Winkle. Harry Houdini's star vehicle *The Man From Beyond* (1922) was perhaps the first hero to spend a hundred years frozen in ice, followed of course by Captain America. The direct inspiration for the mix of Holmesian savvy and comical misunderstanding in these films is most likely Nicholas Meyer's *Time After Time* (which was set in San Francisco and had Malcolm McDowell's H.G. Wells foolishly claim to be Sherlock Holmes).

Given the persistence of the basic idea and the solid mid-list casting, it's a surprise that a series along these lines didn't get made. It may be the BBC had a smart idea in making their adventurer a new character—though an early idea was that Adam Adamant should be Sexton Blake—because they could more effectively balance his dashing, know-it-all qualities with comic or even poignant business about how the world has changed since the days of clear-cut good and evil. *The Return of Sherlock Holmes* repeats a sequence from the *Adam Adamant* pilot in which the hero takes a disconsolate tour of his beloved London and finds it much changed—221B Baker St is now above a McDonalds. In a similar stretch of *Sherlock Holmes Returns*, Holmes, ignoring his carer's warning, barges into an adult bookshop ("I'm an adult") then comes out stunned and unable to speak of what he's seen inside. The problem is that Doyle's Holmes is too well-established as a mercurial, unflappable, worldly-wise character—the sort who'd happily infiltrate an opium den or get engaged to a housemaid while in disguise—to work as a blundering idiot. *Time After Time* had to make Wells considerably prissier than he really was to pull off similar gags and there's a nice bit of subversion in the similarly-toned *Warlock* where a torn-through-time 17th century witchfinder rolls his eyes as a patronizing modern woman assumes he thinks the world is flat. For much of the running time of these films, the revived Holmes seems like a lunatic—indeed, very much like the lunatic heroes who think they're Sherlock Holmes in *They Might Be Giants* or *The Return of the World's Greatest Detective*. The relationships with female Watson characters in those are reprised almost exactly in the two *Returns*—and perhaps serve as a model for the contemporary spin on a crazy English Sherlock and smart American woman Watson in *Elementary*. Of course it turned out that the way to bring Holmes up to date was not to transport him from Victorian England to urban America, but simply to reimagine him as if he were a contemporary character—first, by creating equivalent characters in *The Zero Effect, House* and *Monk*... and then by using Doyle's character names, more obviously in *Sherlock* and *Elementary*. So the defrosted Holmes idea is on ice again... and a modern TV remake of *Time After Time* was cancelled halfway through its run.

The Return of Sherlock Holmes was scripted by Bob Shayne, a long-time TV writer for the likes of *Murder, She Wrote, Hart to Hart* and *Simon & Simon* who would later work on the two Christopher Lee-Patrick MacNee *Sherlock Holmes The Golden Years* TV films. It's reasonably smartly directed by Kevin Connor (*From Beyond the Grave, Motel Hell*) and has a decent mystery drawn loosely from *The Sign of Four*... which gives rise to a slight logistical problem in that Holmes (Michael Pennington) is supposed to have had the career we know about from Doyle, but here runs into a lot of characters with names lifted from the canon and a mystery that parallels one of his most famous cases, but never remarks on the coincidence. Jane Watson (Margaret Colin), descendant of the Good Doctor, operates her own Boston detective agency, which is struggling thanks to her soft-heartedness. To raise funds she has to sell off her only asset—a house in England left in trust by her ancestor, along with a box of documents. In the basement she finds Holmes in a rusty cryo-chamber of his own design—having frozen himself when infected with bubonic plague by a trick puzzle-box sent to him by one of Moriarty's brothers. He hesitates to ask whether the disease is curable now. It is, thanks to big helpfully-labelled boxes of drugs in the local doctor's surgery, though Watson has to spirit the patient away before the doctor can have him committed. With blithe disregard for English geography, the film makes Exmoor, Burnham-on-Sea, and the White Cliffs of Dover within walking distance of each other... but then decamps to America, where Holmes lucks into a case involving a series of murders, a cache of counterfeit money, a long-ago skyjacking and a side trip to Lake Havasu, where he stumbles across London

Bridge (as seen in the time-travelling 1985 Jack the Ripper TV movie *Bridge Across Time*) in the Arizona desert and thinks he's in Heaven.

As was a convention on television for decades, mystery is sabotaged by a prologue that shows who the baddie is and what sort of crookery he's up to. We then spend long acts with the plodding sleuth catching up with an audience who were presumed likely to nod off and so needed to have it all spelled out for them. Here we see Barry Morse—who isn't playing Moriarty or a descendant, but is a great match for Doyle's description of the Napoleon of Crime—doing foul deeds before we even meet Watson and Holmes. Shayne plays things slightly smart by not specifying who Morse actually is playing (he signs his crimes "Small," for what it's worth). Pennington is a little on the bland side as Holmes, earnest and serious but struggling to balance incisive brilliance with a situation where he's often ignorant or pathetic. A set-up joke that develops well has him forced to drive a horseless carriage ("we call it a car") with no instruction. Of course, being Holmes, he works it out logically and is a fine driver (until a truck runs him off the road). Colin is competent but no more as the heroine—Shayne may have been thinking of the bantering sexy 'tec partnerships in *Hart to Hart*, *Remington Steele*, or *Moonlighting*, but this casting doesn't strike those sparks, with a low-wattage simmering attraction barely in a class with *Scarecrow and Mrs. King*. Lila Kaye is "Ms Houston," a sassy combo of Mrs. Hudson and Sam Spade's secretary (we see her reading a Jessica Fletcher novel, crossover fans) and Connie Booth—who'd played a Moriarty-Hudson mix in *The Strange Case of the End of Civilisation as We Know It*—is a chic, sexy, possibly *fatale* Violet Morstan, who frankly upstages Colin's Jane Watson. An array of supporting suspects and interested players has room for William Hootkins, Shane Rimmer, Tony Steedman, Daniel Benzali, and Nicholas Guest (being set up as a series regular third wheel—and given the character name Toby, after the dog).

Sherlock Holmes Returns, written and directed by sf-specialist Kenneth Johnson (*The Bionic Woman*, *The Incredible Hulk*, *V*), is broader, sillier and—it has to be said—more entertaining. Overworked ER doctor Amy Winslow (Debrah Farentino) is on hand when a minor earthquake disrupts power to a San Francisco mansion being looked after by a member of the Hudson family (Joy

Coghill). Amy uses her medical skills to help revive Holmes (Anthony Higgins), who has again frozen himself in the basement—here, to offset boredom and prevent him sliding further into drug addiction. Unlike the well-groomed Pennington, Higgins wakes up as a Ben Gunn-bearded, long-fingernailed loon—and sets the tone for his character by mistaking Dr. Winslow for a nurse. Shaved, but with long hair, the great detective is set loose on the city to go after this generation's Moriarty, James Moriarty Booth (broken-nosed Ken Pogue, who manages a nice mix of thug gang boss and mastermind), and delve into a series of bizarre animal-related murders (involving a tiger, piranhas, beetles, and a snake). He keeps rattling off deductions only to be put in his place by explanations of things he's misunderstood—a commendation from a Little League isn't from an association of grateful dwarves, a uniform he assumes identifies a woman as a prostitute is actually a cheerleader outfit, white residue on a table isn't cocaine but lo-calorie sweetener. He rebuilds his life and practice by fits and starts, recruiting some not-too-nasty street punks as his new Baker Street Irregulars, with Zapper (Mark Adair-Rios) positioned as series regular. Glimpsed in a flashback is future teen star Devon Sawa as the young Booth. The script namedrops famous Victorians from Darwin to Charles Peace but also has groaner gags about a piece of evidence being "America's first Holmes video" or the Irregulars calling Sherlock "homie." There's more running about than actual mystery and it ends by appropriating E.W. Hornung's line about there being "no police like Holmes."

✗

Kim Newman is a prolific, award-winning English writer and editor, who also acts, is a film critic, and a London broadcaster. Of his many novels and stories, one of the most famous is *Anno Dracula*.

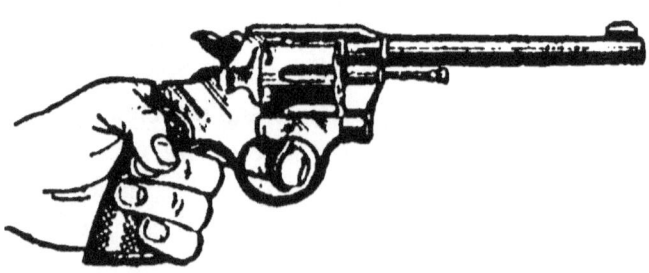

QUAIL, PARTRIDGE, RUBBISH BIRD

by O'Neill Curatolo

There arose a wind sent by the LORD, that drove in quail from the sea and brought them down over the campsite at a height of two cubits from the ground for the distance of a day's journey all around the camp. All the day, all night and all the next day the people gathered in the quail. Even the one who got the least gathered ten homers of them. Then they spread them out all around the camp. But while the meat was still between their teeth, before it could be consumed, the LORD's wrath flared up against the people and he struck them with a very great plague. So that place was named Cibroth-Hatthaava, because it was there that the greedy people were buried.

—Numbers 11:31-34

✗ ✗ ✗ ✗

The common quail (*Coturnix coturnix*) is a plump, tasty treat which has been consumed since ancient times. Associated with the consumption of these birds is a sporadic malady known as coturnism, in modern times described as a form of rhabdomyolysis or muscle damage. Whether coturnism, or simply a case of eating rotten meat, was the basis for the illness described in Numbers will necessarily remain a mystery. However, it has been generally accepted for millennia that quail acquire their toxicity by consumption of poisonous seeds. This was known to the Romans, and Pliny described this danger and its likely cause. Reports of poisoning from eating quail have also occurred throughout the modern era, as recently as 2014 in Turkey.

In the Old World, migratory quail utilize three north-south flyways and therein lies a clue to ancient and modern mysteries about sporadic human maladies after consuming these birds. Large flocks of quail winter in Africa and move north into Europe and western Asia in spring, returning in fall. The eastern flyway crosses the Nile valley, while the western flyway crosses Algeria into France. The central flyway passes northward through Italy. It has been observed that quail can be poisonous during the northward spring migration along the western flyway, but not during the later southward migration. Conversely, quail taking the eastern flyway are not poisonous during the northward spring migration, but become poisonous during the later southward migration. To confound things further, quail which use the central flyway through Italy have not been implicated in food poisonings.

It is generally accepted that quail become toxic due to consumption of poisonous seeds during these migrations. At various times the source of the consumed toxin has been proposed to be hemlock, hellebore, woundwort, and red hempnettle. Only in the case of red hempnettle has scientific investigation resulted in elimination as a possibility. The real plant culprit is not precisely known and perhaps there is more than one, given the observation that the eastern and western flyways become endangered at different times of the year.

Culinary difficulties of this sort are not confined to Europe and Asia Minor. In the 19th century, the American partridge (also called ruffed grouse or pheasant) was a delicacy which unfortunately resulted in occasional "partridge poisoning." While this malady might last for hours to days, it was thankfully not generally fatal. Analogous to European quail coturnism, it is believed that partridge sometimes fed on poisonous mountain laurel, primarily in winter months when snow covered the ground plants they usually preferred. Overhunting and conservation statutes ultimately resulted in almost the entire disappearance of partridge as human food and thus also disappearance of the associated disease.

Rounding out the geographic distribution of this story is the hooded pitohui of New Guinea, also known as the "rubbish bird." The toxicity of this bird is due to the dietary accumulation of homobatrachotoxin, a nerve and muscle poison known also to be present in the skin of "poison-dart frogs" and used at times to poison blowgun darts. In this case, it has been proposed that the rubbish bird acquires the toxin by feeding on Melyrid beetles, which contain various batrachotoxins. Frogs likely similarly ingest this toxin. Humans are rarely sickened by consumption of rubbish birds because these birds have a strong smell and a bitter taste and are not widely eaten. The pitohui gained the nickname rubbish bird for this reason—it is generally useless to the natives of New Guinea.

Armed with all this knowledge, you will now be prepared at your next Gourmand's Club gathering when the waiter says, "Sir, would you fancy the pufferfish? Or perhaps the quail? They are both exquisite. Our chef is a genius with herbs."

For safety's sake I'd choose the quail, but would of course verify that it arrived via the central flyway.

✗

O'Neill Curatolo is a biophysicist who holds 36 US Patents. His suspense novel *Campanilismo* (2013) chronicles the activities of drug industry physicians and scientists in ethically murky waters in New Jersey, Kuala Lumpur, and Malaysian Borneo. He has just published a sequel titled *Too Many Hats: Herbal Medicine and The Mob* (2018), about which Kirkus Reviews said, "An entertaining and illuminating romp through interconnected and delightfully suspect organizations."

THE KRAY TWINS:
A LEGACY OF VIOLENCE
by Peter James Quirk

The East End of London—traditional home of the "Cockney" or working-class Londoner—was almost totally destroyed during World War II.

By the turn of the twentieth century what had been a collection of villages in earlier times: Whitechapel, Mile End, Hackney, Poplar, Hoxton, Bethnal Green, etc., had been gobbled up by London's inexorable and sordid urban sprawl to form a huge Dickensian slum. The majority of its dirt-poor residents, at least those who were more or less honest, made their living on the nearby London docks or sold their wares from barrows in London's street markets—markets such as Petticoat Lane, Portobello Road, Notting Hill Road or Covent Garden.

One would think that life couldn't get more difficult, but when Britain went to war with Hitler's Germany, the *Luftwaffe*, the Nazi air force, irrevocably altered life as the average cockney knew it. Beginning in the summer of 1940, Hitler sent his *Luftwaffe* in wave after wave of bombers over London in an attempt to subdue the British government and subjugate the people's spirit.

Of course the East End with its proximity to the London Docks took the brunt of the bombing. Many thousands of lives were lost and thousands more became homeless, but to compound this, between 1940 and 1945, a whole generation of East-End children—those born in the nineteen thirties—received little to no education. Schools were reduced to rubble along with the houses and those that weren't bombed were commandeered for temporary homeless shelters or army barracks. And the children, often now orphans or at least fatherless, their playgrounds mostly bombed-out houses, were left to fend for themselves and run wild in the streets.

To be sure, the East End always spawned a criminal element, gangs of pick-pockets worked in tandem around large sporting arenas such as horse and dog racing tracks and soccer stadiums. And every neighborhood had its villain or gang of villains: hard men who would fight anyone at the drop of a hat and wouldn't care what happened either to their opponents or themselves. These men lived by their wits and often collected protection money from local pubs and businesses. But what the East End lacked was any real form of organized crime. This essentially ended, however, when the children of the thirties came of age—and in particular, a pair of evil twins born in Hoxton in 1933.

Ronald and Reginald Kray were born to Violet, née Lee, and Charles Kray, a traveling salesman. Just before World War II, the family, which included a brother, Charlie, seven years their senior, moved back to the Lee family compound on Vallence Street, Bethnal Green. The father Charles lived by his wits going door to door all over the southwest of England buying and selling old clothes and jewelry. But when the war came, Charles also became a draft dodger and spent the entire war being hounded by police and consequently was unable to father and discipline his growing brood, as he returned home so infrequently.

The twins, as they came to be called, were influenced in their early childhood by their maternal grandfather, Cannonball Lee, a former boxer and vaudeville entertainer who would do anything for money except actually get a job. And they learned to fight in the streets and in bombed-out buildings, finding themselves supremely suited to this type of warfare. They soon earned a reputation as tough and uncompromising street fighters—all the more hard to beat since they were always together and always defended each other. But at the end of the war they found a new activity, one that thoroughly suited their life-style.

At the annual Victoria Park fair, the twins found themselves at the boxing booth. This was a booth where up-and-coming hard cases could test their mettle by fighting the booth boxers, who were usually retired professional fighters, and if they went the distance they would earn five pounds. This meant the challenger still had to be on his feet after three rounds. Eleven-year-old Ronnie threw his hat into the ring. Of course this challenge was not accepted, but when the ring master explained to Ronnie that he could never find him a suitable opponent, Reggie climbed in the ring and offered to fight his brother. They fought each other to a standstill, entertained the crowd mightily and earned themselves seven shillings and six-pence each, which at the time was roughly a dollar.

Suddenly both Ronnie and Reggie and their relieved parents saw a glimpse of a promising future and they found a trainer—their older brother Charlie, who was already boxing and would spar with them. They both took this training very seriously and made names for themselves as very promising junior prospects. Unnoticed by anyone at the time, though, local street violence was also ratcheting up as the twins took their new-found skills and superior training back to their neighborhood gang. They briefly turned professional, and at one event, all three brothers fought on the same ticket. But since they were now in more and more trouble with local police due to their street violence and general trouble-making, boxing promoters shied away from them, and their careers as prizefighters consequently went nowhere.

In 1952 the twins, now eighteen, were drafted into the army and they reported to the Tower of London, the headquarters of The Royal Fusiliers, an elite infantry regiment. They lasted less than a day, and when they decided that the army was not for them, they knocked their squad corporal out cold and returned home to Bethnal Green. But when they were arrested and returned to the stockade, they received a light punishment since nobody could positively pick out which twin actually struck the squad leader. This incident began what was more or less a running battle between the twins and the military, interspersed by bouts of time served in the stock-ade, until the army finally realized Ronnie and Reggie were never going to become disciplined soldiers and sent them to a final nine months in military prison followed by dishonorable discharges.

The twins, however, learned many valuable lessons during their time in the army. The chief of which was that if they stuck together no matter what, they could defeat anybody, even an institution as tough and uncompromising as the military. They also met and be-friended many other like-minded villains during their stays in the various guard houses, stockades and prisons. This widened their world view as they gradually came to realize that the threat of violence begat fear, and fear bred power and wealth beyond their wildest dreams.

Their first item of business on returning to the East End was to find a headquarters, a hangout. They noticed that all the successful gangsters they met and admired had one, and they found theirs in a former cinema-turned-billiard-hall in Mile End called the Regal. In order to take possession of their dream, they orchestrated a series of fights and disturbances until the manager could take no more and left. They then offered the owner five pounds a week to take it over. The disturbances, of course, ended as quickly and mysteriously as they started.

Now the twins were men of business, making an actual profit, and they took this ascension into the world of commerce quite seriously—they painted the concession stand and recovered those tables that needed it—and soon they were drawing a crowd every night, especially after the pubs closed. Indeed neighborhood toughs were almost afraid not to go there in case they missed any of the crazy stunts and practical jokes the twins would pull—anything from hiring a circus clown to organizing an attack on a rival gang's headquarters, something that Ronnie especially loved to do. He would organize these attacks with an almost military precision, even gathering a coterie of young teenage boys to spy on his targets and map out who would be where and what weapons they would be carrying at the time of the planned attack. His orders were so precise that their gang members—a loose crowd of childhood friends and neighbors known by one and all as "the firm"—took to calling Ronnie "the Colonel."

During the fifties, as everyone grew a little older, the firm began to change. Some of them got married and dropped out of sight, as family and a steady income became a priority in their lives. Their places were taken by more hardened career criminals and toughened thugs the twins met in the army or in jail. Also, the twins's different personalities started to come to the fore.

Ronnie had simple needs; he lived in his mother's house, he didn't know how to steal or gamble, he couldn't even drive a car. He simply loved to fight and absolutely detested the police or any other form of law and order. Reggie, on the other hand, was more reasonable—he was still hell on wheels when it came to fighting—but he had a head for business, and was more agreeable and pleasant to be around. It was he who did the rounds, picking up protection money at all the different businesses in the twins's territory, which at the time encompassed the Mile End, Bethnal Green section of London, just east of Whitechapel. They had not yet attempted to move into the West End, which was where the real money was: in high-end nightclubs, gambling and prostitution. That was to come, although their first attempt didn't work out so well.

Somehow an East End dockworker was able to take over a West End drinking club called The Stragglers. It was a good club but also a popular place for fights, which didn't sit well with the police. Through a friend, however, the owner got in touch with the Kray twins and invited them to become informal partners. This stopped the club fights in a hurry, but also embroiled the twins in other disputes the club owner was engaged in. And eventually Ronnie found himself facing a three-year prison term for causing grievous bodily harm to a member of a rival gang. In November 1956, Ronnie Kray entered Wandsworth Gaol to begin his sentence.

Prison time for Ronnie at first wasn't so terrible. Although he was locked in a single cell from nine-thirty in the evening to six-thirty the following morning, during the day he was surrounded by old lags, friends and acquaintances from the old neighborhood, or from his two years in the army and his interludes in the stockade. All he had to do was learn the rules of prison life and then apply them, with the considerable help from his twin brother on the outside.

Among the inmates of all prisons there is a currency—a forbidden currency, to be sure—and in those days that currency was tobacco. All Ronnie had to do to control this currency was to find married convicts who didn't smoke. For every ounce of tobacco Ronnie received from these men, Reggie would pay the donor's wife one pound. Reggie, being efficient and business-like, always paid these women promptly. With all this surfeit tobacco, Ronnie was able to settle into a fairly comfortable life.

Reggie, too, was making the most of their enforced separation. Now that the Colonel was away, Reggie was able to calm down somewhat and begin to think of more efficient ways to make money. He always believed that the new East End, now much improved thanks to all the post-war rebuilding, needed a West-End-style night club. Several months after Ronnie began his incarceration, Reggie found a derelict building on the Bow Road, which he and a couple of members of the firm fixed up and turned into "The Double R," the first real East End night club.

"The Double R" was a hit almost from the start, and when the twins's older brother Charlie joined forces with Reggie, they opened another club, and then a gambling club right next door to a police station, which included an unlawful bookmaker. Both Reggie and Charlie donned smoking jackets and mingled easily with the crowd—a crowd that now included celebrities and a rich clientele from the West End.

Then, about two years into his three-year jail term, Ronnie was transferred to a minimum-security prison on the Isle of Wight for good behavior. He hated it from the moment he stepped inside—since he was now separated from his friends—and soon began showing definite signs of paranoia. Eventually Ronnie had to be restrained with a straitjacket. He was finally transferred to the mentally-ill wing of Winchester Prison and soon after arriving there he was certified clinically insane.

He was then transferred to an asylum closer to London and treated for schizophrenia. The doctors there believed in treating all their patients equally, even violent convicts such as Ronnie Kray. Ronnie responded well to treatment and soon began acting normally; he was expecting to be sent back to prison to complete his sentence. But when that didn't happen, Reggie decided to take matters in his own hands and break out his brother. This was an old trick that they used before. Reggie visited his twin and Ronnie walked out of the facility wearing Reggie's topcoat. All Reggie had to do to leave after the escape was discovered was to show the staff his driver's license.

He previously arranged to hide Ronnie in a trailer on a farm in the countryside on the other side of London. He paid an old friend of Ronnie's to stay with him and brought him back to Bethnal Green every once in a while for visits, as a reward for Ronnie's good behavior. And as soon as Ronnie stopped exhibiting signs of his schizophrenic paranoia, Reggie persuaded his brother to turn himself in. Of course, since Ronnie had been gone so long, the British court system demanded that his mental state be reevaluated—he passed his tests with ease, and was taken back to Wandsworth to finish his sentence, much to his and the Kray family's satisfaction.

The moment Ronnie Kray was released from Wandsworth was the beginning of a huge change in the family fortunes. At first Reggie and Charlie managed to appease their brother and keep him from interfering with their profit-making enterprises. They gave him all the money he needed, even sent him off into the country on weekends with a trusted friend as a minder. But gradually Ronnie's paranoia got the better of him and he began destroying all the gangland alliances his brothers formed by stirring up battles with old enemies as well as new ones in other sections of London, areas much closer to the West End where the real money—gambling money—lay waiting. He even began collecting large amounts of protection money from a prominent and notorious West End landlord—a man named Peter Rachman. But when one of Rachman's checks to Ronnie bounced and Ronnie began to move in on Rachman's enforcers and rent collectors, Rachman, who was no fool, offered Ronnie a much larger prize to get them off his back: a West End gambling club called Esmerelda's Barn.

At this time Ronnie was temporarily on his own—his twin was doing time for another enforcement deal that had gone horribly wrong, although his lawyers had him out of jail temporarily on a technicality—and while Reggie was away, Ronnie acquired a new friend, Leslie Payne. Payne was not a gangster but a shrewd businessman down on his luck, who understood the possibilities the Kray brothers could bring to cement his shady dealings. He was also very sure of himself in a quiet way that appealed to Ronnie especially. And with a combination of Payne's business savvy and the twins's violent reputation, it wasn't long before Esmerelda's Barn, a veritable gold mine, was under their complete control.

When Ronnie Kray was in Wandsworth Gaol he met and befriended a man named Frank Mitchell, who was known to the British tabloids as the Mad Axe-man. Mitchell, a giant of a man with very limited intelligence, was thirty-two years old and had already spent eighteen of those years behind bars. And although his body was covered in scars from repeated birchings for attacking prison guards, he was in reality a very gentle man when he was treated kindly and with respect. When he was accused of the attempted murder of a fellow inmate, Ronnie, with the fearsome Kray reputation behind him, spread the word that if anyone testified against

Mitchell they would be sorry. Consequently, Frank was acquitted of any charges related to this incident.

Later, when Frank was interred in Dartmoor Prison at Her Majesty's pleasure—i.e., indefinitely—the Kray twins wrote to him regularly and visited him often. By this time, however, Frank found a home for himself. He was treated leniently by the guards and he was even allowed to wander away from work parties to ride wild Dartmoor ponies all over the moors and occasionally stop into a pub or two. He even had a girlfriend, a local school teacher who he used to meet for sex in a local barn. Also the prison warden, who always addressed him by his first name, promised he would try to get him an early release, which is the main reason the Krays did not try to help him escape.

In 1966 they changed their minds, although it is not really certain why they did—they certainly did not need another strong arm; they had all they needed. But before long they had Frank holed up in London, with his minders assisting him in writing letters to the press proclaiming he was being held unfairly. The twins even provided him with a girlfriend, with whom he promptly fell in love. Eventually, however, after he became a problem to handle and keep hidden, he simply disappeared off the face of the earth. Frank Mitchell is officially still the only escaped prisoner from Dartmoor Prison who has never been recaptured.

When Reggie went back to Wandsworth to finish his sentence, he left Ronnie in full possession of one of the finest gaming clubs in London at a time when Parliament had just legalized gambling. (The government had taken this measure hoping it would take the industry away from the criminal element, but what it did in reality was simply legalize their activities.) At first, Ronnie enjoyed dressing up and watching his money roll in, but he soon became bored. It simply didn't seem right to him that he made money without beating someone to a pulp—or at least threatening to do it—although it didn't take long for him to come up with something.

Gaming clubs make their money by being very shrewd judges of character, especially when it comes to extending credit and accepting checks. The manager understood this very well, but when he wasn't around, Ronnie would accept a check from anyone. If it bounced, he didn't care; he simply found the culprit and beat him up, accepting whatever money he could drag out of him.

It didn't take long for the manager, a very shrewd man, to real-ize that the twins, and especially Ronnie, were going to chase their best clients away. So he cut his losses, abandoned his position and began another club, taking his favorite customers with him. This club is still in operation to this day and is what Esmerelda's Barn should have been—a permanent gold mine.

But in the meantime, Ronnie was living the good life and even rented a West End apartment. He was taken everywhere by his rich clients, who enjoyed being seen with a famous gangster—he was even taken to lunch at the House of Lords. And when Reggie finished his sentence at Wandsworth, the twins's fortunes began to peak—they also fell in love.

Reggie's love life was more conventional. While he was out on bail, he met and started dating the sixteen-year-old sister of one of his childhood friends. When he went back to Wandsworth, he began writing to her every day—sometimes even poetry. They eventually married, but the girl found life with Reggie much too stressful and eventually succeeded in committing suicide after several attempts. Ronnie, on the other hand, had long been homosexual, and now even he settled down and moved a beautiful, long-lashed youth into his apartment in the West End.

These distractions, however, seemed to have no effect on their ever-expanding empire. Guided by the watchful eye of their friend Leslie Payne, the twins moved into or had a piece of most of the high-end gambling clubs in London, as well as many other busi-nesses, some even legitimate. All through the first few years of the sixties, their power and, by extension, their finances, grew expo-nentially. That is, until a young detective inspector named Leonard Read, newly transferred to the East End, began taking an interest in them.

The first thing he had to overcome was a scandal that was play-ing out in the national newspapers. In the early sixties, a time when homosexuality was still illegal, *The Daily Mirror*, a left-leaning national tabloid, accused a member of the House of Lords of at-tending gay sex parties with a leading East End gangster, the head of all current protection rackets. They also stated they had pho-tographs to prove their accusations, even though they had been warned not to print them. Rather than suing *The Daily Mirror*, the accused peer, Lord Boothby, wrote a carefully worded letter to *The*

London Times, in which he denied all the charges and dared them to accept the consequences of publishing any photographs.

As it happened, *The Daily Mirror*'s story was largely true and Lord Boothby's letter a tissue of lies, but *The Daily Mirror*, for some reason, backed down and issued an unqualified apology. This meant that the police not only could not hound Lord Boothby and his gay friends, but they also had to be careful investigating the Kray Twins, since Ronnie had been the homosexual gangster mentioned in the story.

Throughout most of the sixties, the twins's power and influence grew. Most new gambling clubs would not think of opening their doors before coming to terms with Reggie, who by all accounts was a reasonable man to deal with—certainly much easier than Ron, who by now was dreaming of running his own murder-for-hire business, and by this time was already responsible for the disappearance of several noted villains. One, a leading member of a rival gang, Ronnie actually shot in the head while he was sitting at the bar of an East End pub. Of course it goes without saying that no one who saw the deed was able to recognize the gunman.

By 1968, however, Detective Inspector Read managed to break through the wall of silence surrounding the twins and amass enough evidence and witnesses willing to testify against them. And in one fell swoop, the twins and almost their entire firm were picked up and charged with two counts of murder, for which both Ronnie and Reggie received thirty years in prison—Reggie for the murder of Jack "The Hat" McVitie, and Ronnie for the shooting of George Cornell in the Blind Beggar pub in Whitechapel.

Jack "The Hat" McVitie was a member of the firm who was contracted out to murder Leslie Payne after Payne and the twins fell out. This was quite possibly due to Ronnie's paranoia, but after Jack was paid £1,500 in advance but was unable to deliver, Ronnie held a gun to his head and pulled the trigger. When the gun jammed, Ronnie held McVitie in a bear hug and handed his brother a kitchen knife. Reggie finished the job. It was rumored that Jack the Hat's liver fell out of his body while he was being stabbed and had to be flushed down the toilet.

George Cornell was a member of a rival gang—the Richardson Brothers gang from South London—who, rumor has it, called Ronnie Kray a fat pouf. Nobody knows for sure if this is true, but the Krays and the Richardsons were at war for many years, which justified his killing in Ronnie's eyes. Cornell was the man Ronnie shot in the head in the Blind Beggar.

Ronald Kray was certified insane while serving his prison sentence, and died of a heart attack in 1995 in Broadmoor Prison for the criminally insane.

Reginald Kray died of pancreatic cancer in 2000 eight weeks after being released from prison on compassionate grounds. He served thirty-two years.

The twins's older brother Charlie served ten years, after being convicted for disposing of Jack the Hat's body. He died of a heart attack in 2000.

The Krays are generally considered the only truly successful organized gangsters whom England ever produced.

Reference: *The Profession of Violence*, by John Pearson.

Peter James Quirk is an author, freelance writer and outdoorsman who spends his winters skiing and snowboarding and his summers hiking, biking and playing tennis. His novel *Trail of Vengeance* has a strong ski theme; indeed, the villain of the story is a disgraced ski instructor. Many of his stories, however, cover World War II and its aftermath. It is a fascinating, if tragic, period to explore, and the villains and heroes are so easy to find.

THE WHOLE ART OF DETECTION

a book review by Eugene D. Goodwin

Holmesians should recognize the title of this book by Lyndsay Faye—it is the same as Sherlock Holmes's magnum opus, which he wrote, I believe, after retiring and becoming a beekeeper. But Ms. Faye's *The Whole Art of Detection* is a collection of fifteen "newly discovered" Holmesian pastiches, following the author's Holmes novel *Dust and Shadow*, another version of the great sleuth's battle to apprehend Jack the Ripper.

Since you are a reader of *Sherlock Holmes Mystery Magazine*, you surely will want to get yourself a copy of Ms. Faye's book, for these are some of the best Holmes stories ever written! They are sorted into four sections: I: Before Baker Street; II: The Early Years; III: The Return; IV: The Later Years. Included are cases alluded to by Dr. Watson—Colonel Warburton's Madness, the Amateur Mendicant Society and, among others (sometimes only alluded to) an ingenious explanation of the disappearance of Mr. James Phillimore… though our editor Mr. Kaye prefers the one he included in his humorous fantasy novel *The Incredible Umbrella* and since the Conan Doyle Estate authorized that version, perhaps it is what actually happened. Perhaps not.

All fifteen of Ms. Faye's tales are good; the ones I enjoyed the most are "The Adventure of the Honest Wife," which includes a particularly nasty husband!, "An Empty House," "The Adventure of the Willow Basket" and "The Adventure of the Mad Baritone."

✗

Gene Goodwin is a fan of Colorado, since that's where he learned to love TexMex food.

THE ADVENTURE OF THE TIRED CAPTAIN

by S. Subramanian

> The July which immediately succeeded my marriage was made memorable by three cases of interest, in which I had the privilege of being associated with Sherlock Holmes and of studying his methods. I find them recorded in my notes under the headings of "The Adventure of the Second Stain," "The Adventure of the Naval Treaty," and "The Adventure of the Tired Captain."
>
> —"The Naval Treaty" (*The Memoirs of Sherlock Holmes*)

In the course of a long and illustrious career, it fell to the lot of my friend Sherlock Holmes to investigate cases of virtually every description and involving virtually every field of human endeavour. Not surprisingly, therefore, his professional work sometimes took him into the arena of the sporting world. A lump of clay, peculiar to the jumping pit of the athletic field in the grounds of a college, proved to be a decisive clue in solving a case which I have recorded elsewhere under the title of "The Three Students." One of Holmes's most notable forensic triumphs was achieved on the racing track of Winchester, a matter I have dealt with in detail in an account I wrote under the heading of "Silver Blaze." Other associations with the sporting life were less fortunate and one in particular, connected to the sport of rugby and which I have documented in one of my memoirs of Holmes as "The Adventure of the Missing Three-Quarter," ended on a most tragic note. What I am about to relate now belongs to the world of cricket, our summer game which—if I may so put it—has been graced for so long by the presence, looming benignly over it, of the peerless Doctor William Gilbert.

It was on a crisp June morning of the year '89, I find recorded in my notebook, that a knock upon the door announced the arrival at our quarters of a fresh-complexioned athletic youth who could not have been more than twenty-one or twenty-two years of age.

"Come in," cried Sherlock Holmes. "Pray be seated and tell us how we may be of service to you. Only you must not seek my advice on the finer points of how to improve your cricket. Though I love the game, I have no particular proficiency in it—unlike Dr Watson here who, in his time, has played for the Edinburgh University Eleven. Tut, young man, there is no cause for that startled look upon your face. It calls for no great powers of divination to recognize a cricketer in an athletic youth who, in his urgent anxiety to consult a detective, has so far forgotten himself as not to change his white flannels and spiked cricketing boots before setting out upon his mission. So please tell me how I may help you, remembering only that I am unlikely to be of the least assistance in pronouncing on how one may deliver a ball that spins the other way while purporting to be a leg-break: the person for that, I understand, would be a boy in Eton College called Rosanquet."

'No, sir," said the young man, with a good-humoured laugh. "I am not here to consult you on the 'Rosie,' but on a matter which is arguably a good deal more serious."

"You have my undivided attention," said Holmes.

"You must know then, Mr Holmes," said our visitor, "that my name is Lionel Balairet and that I am a student of Waldham College at the University of Fordbridge, which I have the honour of representing on the field of cricket as a member of its Playing XI. I am here on the insistence of several of my team-mates to seek your assistance and advice on how to get one particular member of the team, C.B. Wry, to turn out for the crucial match against Somerset, to be played tomorrow at the University Parks. He has taken to his bed in what appears to be a state of complete and unexplained prostration and refuses to entertain our impassioned entreaties not to let the team down."

"Ah! The details, now, please. While I take a sufficient interest in cricket to be aware of the existence of Mr Wry, I need rather more information about him and the events surrounding his present condition if I am to be of any use in the matter."

"I understand that, Mr Holmes. Let me try to tell you what little I know of Wry and his present situation. Wry must be one of the most completely accomplished sportsmen that Fordbridge has ever known in its history, apart also from being an outstanding scholar. He came to Fordbridge from Repton School in Derbyshire (where

I studied myself, as had my younger brother, also a cricketer). Wry was a prodigious Classics scholar, winning several prizes for both prose and verse in both Latin and Greek. He represented the School in football and was also its cricket captain. It is out of worry for this now tired captain, as *his* captain in the Fordbridge team, that I present his case before you, Mr Holmes.

"Wry came to Fordbridge on a scholarship. His father, Mr Lewis Wry, was once a person of means, but he fell upon hard times and the family's fortunes have been gradually whittled away by dwindling property prices. It is hard for young Wry to maintain himself in the comforts of a typical undergraduate gentleman."

"And yet he contrives to do so?" enquired Holmes.

"Yes, he contrives, Mr Holmes."

"By what means, may I ask?"

"Well, he earns some money from private tuition and also from his writing: he has already written for *Wisden*, for instance."

"And what, pray, are his other sources, Mr Balairet?"

"Why, none that I know of, Mr Holmes."

"Come, come, Mr Balairet, you cannot expect me to help you if you will insist on being reticent with the truth. For the successful prosecution of his job, data are as essential for the investigator as the right equipment is for a cricketer: I cannot make inferences without facts any more than you can make runs without a bat. I would urge you most strenuously, my dear young man, to come clean with me. Failing that, it should be quite impossible for me to deal with this case."

"My apologies to you, Mr Holmes: it was not my intention to mislead you; it is just that I did not wish to seem, even to myself, to be disloyal to my friend. I see now that that is quite the wrong way of viewing the matter. In response to your specific query: a major source of Wry's finances has been borrowing. He is in considerable debt."

"Ah! Just as I imagined. You see, Mr Balairet, I have been up at Fordbridge myself in my youth and so am not entirely unaware of the travails of relatively indigent scholars there. But pray proceed. How has Mr Wry been faring at Fordbridge?"

"In all other respects, exceptionally well. Academically, he recently performed outstandingly in his Classical Moderations. He has a Fordbridge blue in each of cricket, football and athletics.

He has just broken the British and equalled the world record for the long jump. He is an outstanding batsman, set fair to be England's greatest batsman in the not-too-distant future (alongside, I might add, his brilliant Camford contemporary, the Indian prince and batting prodigy Sinjhi). He can also turn his arm over in the cause of some fast-medium bowling. He is quite the life and soul of any party: one of his favourite stunts is to crouch in front of a mantelpiece, jump straight up in the air from his crouch, turn around at the height of his ascent and land on the mantelpiece, facing you! Wry is a wonderfully popular man and the rising star of the day in every way. *Vanity Fair* described him in these terms in a recent article published in the magazine: 'He is sometimes known as "C.B."; but it has lately been suggested that he should be called "Charles III."'"

"What seems to be the problem, then?"

"Why, Mr Holmes," cried Balairet, "it is the man's cursed tiredness, which seems to have descended quite suddenly upon him, in the course of the last two days and laid him low. He cowers in bed all day long and will refuse to consider playing in tomorrow's match against Somerset, and, indeed, to participate in any of the routine events of everyday life."

"This seems to be a case for a physician."

"He absolutely refuses to see one."

Holmes shot an enquiring look in my direction.

"It is hard to form a snap judgement, Holmes, without the benefit of a clinical examination," I said. "But from what Mr Balairet tells us, it appears to be a classic case of shattered nerves. Our cousins across the Atlantic are prone to describe the condition as one of 'neurasthenia,' though our own typical Harley Street alienist would be inclined to certify it as a nervous breakdown, plain and simple. It is the sort of thing that might be expected to be brought on by an underlying melancholia caused by some longstanding, nagging worry—a condition that can be concealed over a long time with more or less success, as much from others as from oneself, until a sudden crisis precipitates a complete and comprehensive nervous prostration accompanied by physical lassitude and mental paralysis, such as seems to describe the present situation of Mr Wry."

"That is most instructive, Watson—especially the bit about the 'sudden crisis.' From what you tell us, Mr Balairet, the manifestation of Wry's dramatic symptoms of complete fatigue can be dated to a couple of days ago. Can you try to think back to any specific event to which your friend's collapse can be linked?"

Our client knit his brows in thought before his face suddenly cleared up as at the triggering of some recollection. "Why, Mr Holmes, now that you mention it, I am suddenly reminded of what Billson, our opening bowler, told me yesterday. As he was leaving the science laboratory two evenings ago—Billson is a Natural Sciences man—he was accosted by a couple of rude-looking men at the gate of the lab and entrusted with an envelope with the instruction to make sure that his 'colleague at the lab,' C.B. Wry, received it straightaway—"

"'Colleague at the lab'?" echoed Holmes.

"Wry has been known to visit the laboratory from time to time."

"What business does a man researching Thucydides have in a science laboratory?"

"I am sure I don't know, Mr Holmes."

"Never mind. And did your fast bowler hand over that missive to Wry?"

"He did indeed, Mr Holmes."

"A final question. Is Wry known to have any romantic attachment?"

"Well, it is no secret that he has a rather powerful 'crush' on one of his fellow-undergraduates, a Miss Lisa Hopkins. I'm afraid the affair is somewhat one-sided and Wry's unrewarded pursuit of the object of his affections is a matter of some general amusement for his friends."

"Thank you, Mr Balairet. Yours has been an admirably clear deposition and it is time for us now to take some concrete steps in the matter. The problem is an elementary one and my mind is more or less made up on what the source of the difficulty is. What is wanting are the details of the case, on the basis of which we may formulate a plan of action. I suggest we return together to Fordbridge and that you arrange for us to meet Wry there. Watson, may I suggest you equip yourself with the heaviest stick in your possession? I propose to do the same myself, for I do not rule out the prospect of violence as this case unfolds. I also propose to carry with me some of the interesting products of his trade which we managed to lay our hands on when we took in Archie Stamford, the forger, near Farnham. Something tells me they will come in handy. Come! To St Pancras now and thence to Fordbridge."

⚡ ⚡ ⚡ ⚡

Arrived at Waldham College, Lionel Balairet guided us to C.B. Wry's lodgings, which entailed climbing up the dark and winding staircase of a building in the College quadrangle. A knock on the door elicited no response and the second knock met with the same fate.

"This is Balairet here, Wry, and I am accompanied by Mr Sherlock Holmes and Dr John Watson of Baker Street, London. Mr Holmes is an eminent consulting detective and he has consented to come here in order to help you. Please open up, old man."

At last we had a response, but a far from encouraging one: a testy voice from within the room said tersely, "The lot of you can go to blazes."

Balairet looked at us with a helpless expression on his face and was about to say something through the closed door when Holmes laid a finger to his lips and murmured: "I believe this should fetch us an *entrée*." Tearing out a sheet of paper from a pocketbook, he scribbled a message with the stump of a pencil. Looking over his shoulder, I read this short communication:

> We are here to try to recover that photo. It is the only thing to do. Kindly cooperate, in your own interest.

He then slipped the notepaper into the room from under the door, as we awaited developments—for which, in the event, we did not have to wait long. The door opened and a youth of considerable physical beauty, the classical type of a Greek god, bade us enter.

"Thank you, Mr Balairet, I think we will take it from here," said Holmes.

The young man looked very relieved to be spared any further involvement in the matter and with a cheery "Good luck, Wry, old chap," he vanished from the scene.

Wry's room was a typical example of the untidy trappings of a Fordbridge undergraduate's study, with books and papers littered about the desk and bookshelves, the walls lined with pictures of cricketers and characters from Greek mythology and a corner of the room cluttered with cricketing gear, including a bat, a pair of gloves and a pad, the whole pervaded by a strong smell of linseed oil with which cricketers are wont to season their bats.

The young man motioned to us to sit down while himself taking the edge of his cot. He buried his head in his hands and groaned: "How do you know about the photo, Mr Holmes?"

"It wasn't so much knowledge as educated speculation, Mr Wry," responded Holmes. "I am glad to learn that my inference has not been misplaced. As I was telling your friend Mr Balairet, I have been up at Fordbridge myself and am therefore quite well acquainted with the stresses to which scholars of limited financial means are subjected. When I learnt that you were up to your neck in debt despite earning what you could from tutoring and writing, it occurred to me that there must be other sources of income, very likely of a somewhat compromising nature, that you might have tried to exploit."

"What did you have in mind, Holmes?" I asked.

"Watson, when I heard about a Classics scholar's occasional visits to the science laboratory, my speculation was deflected pronouncedly more in the direction of certainty. As a former Natural Sciences man myself, I am aware of the fact that science laboratories in the University often employ the services of male models, posing *au naturel*, for use in demonstrations of the male anatomy. This was no very far-fetched possibility to imagine in your case, Mr Wry, knowing, as I did, that you are a splendid athlete with an exquisitely proportioned body—of which I now have visual confirmation. For myself, I entertain no objection to this practice and rather see it as an admirable contribution to the pedagogical devices of instruction in science. But it is unreasonable to expect most other people to view the issue with my own somewhat bohemian and liberal perspective on such matters. I daresay, in particular, that it is not the sort of thing that would go down very well with one such as, shall we say, Miss Lisa Hopkins—ah! I see that the arrow has found its mark!"

"Mr Holmes, you must be a wizard!" said the cricketer, blushing to the roots of his fair hair.

"I can no more admit to being a wizard than Dr Johnson could admit to being a philosopher! At best, a student of human nature, as in the good Doctor's case, shall we say? However that may be, I realized that your abrupt collapse a couple of days ago, coming on top of all the other strains of your straitened existence, argued the case in favour of a sudden crisis in your affairs. I had confirmation of that hypothesis from Balairet's account of the letter delivered through your team-mate Billson. That it had its origin in the science laboratory pointed again in the direction of an instance of nude modelling for scientific instruction. That, coupled with the effect the letter has apparently had on you, together with a consideration of what a revelation of the facts of the case could do to your (already difficult) relationship with your young lady, hinted strongly at blackmail as the source of the sudden and apparently irredeemable tiredness of Repton's former captain."

"How bad is the situation, Mr Holmes?"

"Ah! That depends crucially on who is in possession of the negatives of your photographs. I can only hope that you have, on all occasions, observed the precaution of taking sole possession of the negatives. Failing that, things could go very badly with us."

"Mr Holmes, I admit I have been every kind of damned fool in this affair; but I am happy to say that I've at least had the good sense of keeping the negatives of all the photographs in my own sole custody. The anatomist, you see, is a close friend of mine and a keen amateur photographer: he develops all the photos himself and on every occasion he has passed on the negative to me immediately after developing it."

"That is indeed a stroke of great good fortune."

"But how did all this come to pass, Mr Holmes?"

"Through carelessness," said Holmes in a tone of profound annoyance. "It is all very well for the sponsors of your modelling to claim the virtues of the scientific temper in their defence, but I am quite without sympathy for their complete lack of ordinary discretion and prudence in the way they conduct their business. For one thing, it would make a good deal of sense for the photographs of the models to have the models's faces blocked off. For another, the pictures of models should be preserved securely and out of reach of harm's way. It is clear, in this case, that a photograph has been left lying around carelessly for some laboratory assistant in need of ready cash to convert it to his advantage by selling it to a known blackmailer or his agents. My own suspicions in the matter point in the direction of a particularly vicious specimen of humanity who rejoices in the name of Charles Augustus Milverton, a man whose entire career has been built on the ransomed ruins of the lives of others. By the way, have you preserved a copy of the blackmail note that was brought to you by Billson?"

"Here it is, sir," said Wry, extracting a crumpled note from an envelope in his pocket.

Holmes examined both the note and the envelope minutely.

"Cheap note-paper, cheap envelope, nothing of any particular interest in these. And what does the message say? Ah, an illiterate scrawl in capitals:

> WE HAVE A COPY OF YOUR PHOTO IN THE AL-TOGETHER. IF YOU DO NOT WANT IT TO BE SENT TO MISS LISA HOPKINS, COME TO THE 'COCK AND BULL' PUBLIC HOUSE AT 6 P.M. ON THE 8TH. THREE OF US WILL BE WAITING FOR YOU. THE PHOTO WILL BE HANDED OVER TO YOU IN EXCHANGE FOR £200. COME ALONE. NO TRICKS.

Well, well, this is explicit enough. What do you propose to do about it, Wry?"

"I am ruined, Mr Holmes," cried the wretched youth. "What can I do?"

"Display a little more resolve, to begin with," said Holmes, firmly but not unkindly. "It is to our advantage that these scoundrels do not have access to the negative of the photograph. You will pay for the photo, of course, and recover it in your possession."

"It will cost me £200, Mr Holmes! Where am I to find the money, on top of all my other outstanding liabilities?"

"Oh, I have come prepared for that," said Holmes smoothly. "Here are the 200 pounds in crisp ten-pound notes. Don't look so startled, Wry. These are counterfeit notes, the creative endeavour of Archie Stamford the forger of infamous memory, whom Watson and I took near Farnham some years ago, along with some of his productions. Doubtless my possession of these notes is illegal, but it is all in a good cause. Stamford was a dedicated artist and it should take the villains some time to recognize that these notes are forged. But if and when that recognition dawns on them, we should be prepared for a scrap. How long to the Cock and Bull from here?"

"Half-an-hour on foot."

'Very well. It is just getting on to five of the evening now. You are expected to be at the Cock and Bull by six. Watson and I will start out straightaway for the public house. We should be there by half-past-five and will spend an inconspicuous half-hour there exchanging pleasant conversation over a couple of pints of beer while awaiting your arrival. Once you have arrived and the exchange has been effected, we will join you. As I said, we should be prepared for a roughhouse. Dr Watson here is an old campaigner. And you, Wry? Are you ready and willing?"

"Mr Holmes, I shall be delighted to give as good as I get," responded the cricketer, with a grin flitting across his face for the first time that evening.

"Splendid, my dear fellow! Come Watson, let us get on with it."

⚹   ⚹   ⚹   ⚹

Both Holmes and I were glad for an opportunity to stretch our legs and we set out briskly when we realized we hadn't sought directions to our destination.

"Most public houses in Fordbridge are of respectable antiquity and unless the Cock and Bull has emerged after my time, I should be able to recall where it is, given that I had come to acquire a reasonably intimate acquaintance with the public houses of Fordbridge during my tenure here. Let me think. Ah, it comes back to me now. I know exactly where it is. Come with me, Watson!"

With unerring accuracy, Holmes led me through a bewildering maze of cross-streets and alleyways and in just under a half-hour, we found ourselves at the establishment called the Cock and Bull. We seated ourselves at a table affording a convenient view of the main door and ordered a pint of bitter each.

"Don't look now," said Holmes in a low voice, "but if I am not much mistaken, those three thoroughly unsavoury-looking characters at the landlord's bar should be our men."

And so they turned out to be, for they started walking toward the door when, upon the dot of six o'clock, our young friend Wry hove into view. There was a short exchange of conversation between him and the leader of the three men before the money for his photograph was exchanged by the cricketer with the leader. Wry pocketed the photo and started walking away rapidly, even as we paid for our drinks and followed him swiftly out into the street. No sooner had we joined him than there was an outraged bellow that carried to us from the direction of the gang of three.

"'Ere," shouted the leader, "These notes is fake. 'Ang on there a second, will yer, yer welching dorg?"

And with that the three ruffians were upon us. Holmes took on the leader while Wry and I dealt with the other two. Perhaps it is because we were prepared, perhaps it is because we were in a state of high-strung anticipation, perhaps it is because each of us was filled with righteous anger, or perhaps and most likely, it was a combination of all three factors. What I do know is that we waded most vigorously into our adversaries and after knocking the sticks out of their hands with ours, it was a matter of bare knuckles and fists. Before long the gang had taken to their heels and we had good reason to believe that among ourselves we had accounted for one cheek-bone, one nose and one jaw.

"Why, Mr Holmes," said our young friend, holding his sides in delighted laughter, "that is the most glorious piece of action I have seen in a long time!"

"Yes, I will not deny that the incident was refreshing," smiled Holmes. "I trust you are not the worse for wear, Watson?"

"Nothing that a cold joint of steak applied to the knuckles will not cure," I replied happily.

"Splendid!" said Holmes. "I take it you have your photograph back, Wry? Guard it well. As for myself, I managed to wrest Archie's ill-begotten notes back from that ruffian: one never knows when they may not be of assistance again. Well, all's well that ends well; and I trust we may take it that we have succeeded in bringing to a satisfactory conclusion the Adventure of the Tired Captain?"

"A former captain, Mr Holmes, of Repton; and with luck, a future captain of Fordbridge after old Balairet passes out this year. And most definitely no longer tired. How can I ever thank you enough for your many kindnesses, leave alone repay you for your professional services?"

"As I have had occasion to clarify to other clients, the fee for my professional services is on an unvarying scale, save when I choose to remit it altogether, as I do on this occasion: I do not charge clients who are students. As for repaying Watson and my alleged kindnesses, we shall both feel amply rewarded if you should turn out for that game against Somerset tomorrow."

"Mr Holmes, Dr Watson, I promise you I will do the best I can. And I will never forget what you two have done for me today."

⚡   ⚡   ⚡   ⚡

It was late that evening when we found ourselves back at our lodgings in London and it was with not a little gratitude—ravenous as we were from our travel, from our exertions of the day and from the long hours that separated us from our last meal—that we addressed the excellent cold supper which Mrs Hudson laid out for us. For some time after we ingested the eminently satisfying meal, we sat comfortably stretched out in our respective armchairs, smoking our respective pipes peaceably and in silence. Eventually—for it was a matter that had assumed the shape of a niggling nuisance for some time at the back of my mind—I broke the silence.

"Tell me, Holmes," said I. "I am curious to know: I am aware of how committed you are to every problem which you undertake to examine, but in this instance you have gone far beyond the normal line of duty, by incurring personal expenditure on the case, waiving your fee and risking your own personal, physical safety. Pray why?"

Holmes puffed meditatively at his pipe for some time before replying.

"Well, Watson," he said, "I hadn't thought of it in those terms myself until you brought it up and your question has compelled me to contemplate self-consciously on the motive for the way in which I responded to this case. I should not normally speak with ease of those emotions that stir me deeply, but you touch a chord somewhere with your question and you are, after all, my oldest—perhaps, indeed, my only—friend, and that makes it a great deal less difficult than it normally would be for me to speak of my inmost thoughts.

"In your chronicles of my little exploits, you have often portrayed me as a crusader against crime. But 'crime' is a somewhat formal, legal and rule-book-ridden notion—one which I do not always find particularly appealing, nor convincing. For instance, homo-erotic love is against the law, whereas, between us, I see it only as 'the love that dare not speak its name,' as an affect or emotion or act that lies within the sacred private domain of consenting adults—one which the law, with the support of an illiberal and busy-bodied popular opinion, has seen fit to drag into the sordid glaring light of publicity. Similarly, in the statute-book, murder is murder; but in my book, deliberate, cold-blooded murder for gain is a very different proposition from a murder committed, in the heat of the moment, to protect the honour of a woman. You will recall that we have ourselves, from time to time, taken the law into our own hands, to judge the substantive guilt or otherwise of those that we have discovered to be formally guilty of a crime.

"So, no: I am no crusader against crime. A crusader against sin, then? No, no, Watson, that is too large a quantity for me to handle! I am no theologian and heaven rescue me from the temptation of forever passing judgement on what does or does not constitute the sins of humanity! If I am against neither crime nor sin, then what is it, in my chosen profession, that I fight against? If I were compelled to seek a formal term for it—as your question now compels me to—I would be inclined to suggest that what I seek to fight (with all my imperfections and infirmities ranged against me!) is the perpetration of what one might call a 'moral offence.'

"And of all the moral offences I can think of, the one I have, from an early age, found to be most deeply repugnant to my ethical sensibility is the offence of blackmail. It is a cold and ruthless and parasitical and cowardly and despicable offence, unnatural in the animal kingdom and unique to the human species. I have seen the pathetic effect of blackmail upon its hapless victims—of how their minor peccadillos and private indiscretions have been turned against them in the cause of their mental and material disintegration and in that of the blackmailer's squalid gain.

"I have seen it early in my career and too often for it not to have left its mark on me as a moral offence that I will always fight against, tooth and nail and to the bitter end. I encountered it first, you will remember, in the affair you have described as the adventure of the *Gloria Scott* and the effect wrought by that repugnant blackmailer Hudson upon the father of my friend Victor Trevor from my 'Varsity days. In the matter of 'The Scandal in Bohemia,' I agreed to take on the case, despite my instinctive dislike of my client the King of Bohemia, only because of my opposition to the act of blackmail which I thought that woman was threatening the King with: it was only later that I discovered that Irene Adler was employing that photograph purely for reasons of self-protection and not for reasons of realizing a profit from the foibles of another. It is my deep-seated opposition to blackmail, again, which caused me to break the thread of my investigation into the affair of the Baskerville Hound: you will recall that, in the midst of that case, I had to decline Sir Henry Baskerville's invitation to visit Baskerville Hall on these grounds: 'it is impossible for me to be absent from London for an indefinite time. At the present instant one of the most revered names in England is being besmirched by a blackmailer and only I can stop a disastrous scandal. You will see how impossible it is for me to go to Dartmoor.'

"And so in the case we have just disposed of, Watson. Here is a brilliant and accomplished young man on the threshold of a wonderful life of sport or scholarship or both, threatened with being bled for an act which is, at worst, a minor foolishness. Above all, every one of my instincts rebelled against the horror and slime of a situation in which the game of cricket was threatened by vileness. You know me well, Watson; and I believe I am the last man you would associate with harbouring romantic illusions about the nature of the world we live in. But that does not mean that I hold nothing sacred. Least of all cricket, a game as much as an institution, which is supposed to be associated with the notion of 'fair play' conducted according to rules by which gentlemen abide.

"And I am not so lacking in a knowledge of either history or contemporary affairs as not to be moved by the names of those great sons of Hambledon—Billy Beldham and Noah Mann and the Nyrens, *père et fils*, and Tom Shuter of Hampshire—or, in our own times, the prodigious Dr Grace, not to mention those dour limpets Hornby and Barlow and surely a host of others. Honest, simple, sturdy men, Watson; and geniuses of their craft. Theirs is not the world that one can idly sit by and watch unmoved, even as it is defiled by the depravities of blackmail and extortion.

"I am not a rich man. Even so, some expense out of the personal wallet, the waiving of a fee from a deserving and impecunious student and the sheer pleasure of visiting a broken jaw upon a villain (even if I ran the risk that he might well have visited the same gift upon me)—these struck me as a minor price to pay in a fight against what I judge to be the most ignoble moral offence of which a human being is capable—and one, furthermore, which is perpetrated against a young man who is a supremely gifted artist in a sport that still stands, in a world gone increasingly cynical, for something of grace and honour and skill and chivalry and innocence. Would you view my explanation with sympathy, Watson?"

"Why, no, Holmes," I replied. "With a good deal more than sympathy: with, indeed, the greatest conviction of moral and emotional approval of your position!"

"Good old Watson," said Holmes softly. "You are the one fixed point in a changing world. Stout fellow!"

✗   ✗   ✗   ✗

It was three days later, after Mrs Hudson cleared away the remains of our breakfast, when Holmes tossed across a note to me with these words:

"This arrived a little earlier by the post, Watson. I think you will agree that it constitutes a charming postscript to our intriguing little case of the tired captain—one which also affords a certain light relief from the somewhat solemn note on which we ended our discussion of the matter three nights ago."

The note read as follows:

Waldham College,
Fordbridge

June 11, 1889

Dear Mr Holmes and Dr Watson,

Please accept as an infinitesimal token of my repayment of an irredeemable debt of gratitude to both of you the following extract from the score-card of a cricket match which occurred on June 9th and 10th:

Fordbridge University v Somerset (University Match 1889, played at the University Parks, Fordbridge on 9th and 10th June 1889)

Result: Fordbridge University won by 7 wickets
Fordbridge University first innings
C B Wry   lbw b Styler   110

My friend Lionel Balairet conveys his deeply-felt thanks and respectful regards to you.

With inestimable gratitude and admiration,

I remain,

Yours most sincerely:
C B Wry

S. Subramanian is a retired professor of Economics and otherwise harmless. He is indebted to Arunabha Sengupta for helpful advice on an earlier version of this piece. Wikipedia has been an invaluable source of biographical material on the (fictionalized) cricketers featured in the story.

WHAT WOULD PACINO DO?

by Steve Shrott

"I'm going to kill you. Gonna watch you die and enjoy it. When you leaked that evidence about me, you made a big mistake. And now you're gonna pay." Jonathan Levy moved the gun closer to the bald man.

The bald man's face remained blank. "Thanks. You can go now."

"But I've got more lines."

"I've heard enough." The bald man, whose name was William Henry, wrote something down on a pad, then pushed his chair toward the desk.

Levy didn't move.

"Sir, I have other people to see."

Levy looked around the large empty audition hall, then leaned toward Henry, his small frame tiny next to the other man's meatier physique. "What did you think?"

"Fine."

"I can do it another way if you like. More innocence, add in some humor, tougher. Any way you want."

Henry blew out air. "You should go home, wait for your agent's call."

Levy nodded, sure the casting director gave him a signal—a signal that meant he got the part. That was good news, as he needed the money. He grinned at Henry and left.

✗   ✗   ✗   ✗

Levy had been working in "the biz," as he called it, for several years. He got the odd role, but not enough to keep him from being a waiter in a family restaurant. He hated the rude customers and screaming kids who often spilled ketchup and other crap on his white uniform. He hoped this would be the part that would take him to the top—perhaps getting him work with Pacino, his idol.

In between taking care of his tables Levy called his agent several times, but it always went to voice mail. So later in the day after his shift at the restaurant he headed to the agent's office.

The office was small with dozens of autographed pictures of famous actors on the wall. None of whom his agent Bernie Weber had actually met.

Bernie sat behind his large desk covered with coffee-stained scripts, eating a tuna sandwich. He shook his head. "Sorry."

"I didn't get it?"

Bernie tossed the rest of his sandwich onto a plate. "No."

Levy stared at him, not wanting to believe what he was hearing, even though he'd been rejected innumerable times before. "What did he say?"

"Nothing."

"He must have said something. It was my best audition yet."

Bernie swallowed as though he was trying to get an awful taste down his throat. "He said he didn't believe you could actually kill a man."

Levy's eyes opened wide. "What?"

Bernie moved the plate with the half-eaten sandwich off to one side of his desk. "He said it didn't seem… authentic. That's the word he used."

Levy started to breathe heavily. He'd worked on that scene for days, watching movies, TV shows, reading books about gangsters. Still, the casting director didn't think it was good enough. How was that possible?

"Don't worry about it. I'll have some 'extra' work for you in a few days."

Levy didn't want any damn 'extra' work. He was tired of being a second rater, not getting those big juicy Hollywood roles. He was as good as anyone, better than most. This was his first chance at a decent part in the last six months and he was damn well going to get it. "Did they choose anyone yet, Bernie?"

"Deadline's end of the week."

"Get me another audition with them."

Bernie spread his hands. "I don't know if they're going to go for—"

"Please."

Bernie looked at Levy's hopeful face and blew out air. "I'll see what I can do."

✗ ✗ ✗ ✗

Levy took the subway home as he always did. He usually fell asleep, but this evening he was wide awake, thinking about how to make the audition better. His phone rang and interrupted his thoughts.

"It's Bernie. They said you could come tomorrow at ten-thirty."

"Great. Thanks."

"Don't louse this up. I really had to convince them you were worth seeing again."

"I won't," Levy said, sounding surer than he felt.

He put his phone away and continued thinking about the audition. Whenever he was in a quandary about the biz, he asked himself, what would Pacino do? The answer came quickly.

He'd contact an expert to help him nail things down.

And Levy knew just the expert.

✗ ✗ ✗ ✗

He headed down to the train station and got a ticket for New Haven, where his Uncle Earl lived. Earl had been married for a few years to Levy's aunt—that was, until she disappeared. The police looked into it, but never figured out what happened to her. Levy's dad assumed Earl was behind it. According to rumors, he'd been involved with the mob.

Levy took a taxi to Vaughn Avenue. He walked past the kids playing baseball on the street and marched up the driveway to the white and pink house. It looked like every other home in the suburban area—peeling paint on the trim, a few broken bricks, a torn screen door. Yet something about it gave off an ominous vibe. Levy knocked and waited. When his aunt went missing, the family stopped talking to Earl, and Levy didn't remember ever actually having met him. He just hoped Earl would be willing to help.

A slight older man opened the door, his posture stooped, his face weathered with those under-eye bags that older men got. Levy assumed when you reached a certain age, sleep was a bitch.

"Hi, I'm Jonathan Levy. You know, Larry's son. I—"

Earl's brow creased, his eyes staring at Levy as if he were a wasp Earl was about to swat. "What do you want?"

Levy looked at the man, who now seemed tougher than he imagined and stepped from foot to foot, unsure he'd made the right decision coming here. "I... I need a favor."

Earl grimaced. "Favor? Why the crap would you come here? Your dad and me haven't talked in years."

Levy licked his dry lips, started speaking fast. "I want you to teach me how to kill someone."

Earl crunched his eyebrows together, then a moment later started laughing. "What the hell is this, some joke?"

He was about to shut the door when Levy somehow got out the words he wanted to say—but was equally afraid of saying. "My... my dad told me what you did to Sam Reynolds."

Earl froze, his face hardening.

"He told me that one night the two of you got pissed-drunk and you blurted out that you buried Reynolds's body in the wooded area next to Interstate 9."

Earl grabbed Levy's shirt collar and pulled him toward his face like a tiger about to chomp off the head of a gazelle. Levy could feel the old man's hot breath.

"What you gonna do with that, kid?"

Levy couldn't stop himself. "I, uh, mig-might tell the c-cops."

Earl's other hand reached into his back pocket.

Levy's body trembled as he readied himself to be shot.

Earl's hand came forward. It held a handkerchief. Earl wiped his brow and let Levy go. Then he turned away and walked inside.

Levy's breathing returned to normal. He stared after Earl, not knowing what to make of this—Earl left the door open.

Was he inviting Levy in?

Levy took a chance, walked inside. There he saw a large living room with pictures of nature scenes on several of the walls: a dog sitting on a country road, a grassy hillside, some cows meandering around a waterfall. Odd pictures for a mobster.

Against one of the walls was a leather couch where Earl sat, one leg lying on a hassock.

"Bad arthritis."

Levy nodded, slowly, carefully, moving toward a nearby chair. He sat down gently.

Earl looked at him, his expression softer now. "You know, I like you, kid. You got cajones."

Levy smiled. "So you'll help me?"

"Teach you how to kill someone?"

"I gotta know how it feels. I wanna be in this movie and—"

"Movie? Oh, yeah, the actor. I remember your dad talking about how that's all you ever wanted to be—an actor. As I recall, he and your mother weren't so happy about it."

"They wanted me to be a doctor. But it's just not my—" Levy noticed Earl's eyes drifting away from him and toward the window.

"Oh, crap."

"What?"

Earl heaved himself off the couch, limped out the door. Levy heard yelling but could only make out one phrase—

"Gonna kill you, Warwick." It came from Earl.

A moment later, Earl came back inside, his face red, his breath coming in short gasps. "Stupid bastard."

He sat back down on the couch.

"So will you help me, Uncle Earl?"

"Huh?"

"You know the acting thing. Show me how to look like I'm a killer."

Earl thought a moment. "Yeah, yeah, sure." He stood up and hobbled over to a cabinet.

He reached into a drawer and removed a gun, pushed it into Levy's hand. "Take this."

Levy's body started trembling. "I… I don't need a real gun. I'm only using a fake one in the scene."

"That's crap. If you want it to look real, you have to use real weapons. That's what gives you the power—knowing that with just one shot you can rid the world of any scum you want."

Levy moved the gun from hand to hand, felt the weight, the strength, the power.

"When you're a killer, you're superhuman. You have no fear, no doubt. You look at everyone like they're a piece of garbage, 'cause you never know when you're gonna have to take them out." Earl's leg faltered, and he stumbled. He quickly stuck his arm against the wall and regained his balance. "Killers only got one rule. A favor given is a favor paid. Got it?"

Levy wasn't sure what he was supposed to get, but nodded just the same.

Earl showed him how to hold a gun, how to stand, how to shoot.

After an hour, Levy decided he knew enough to ace the audition. "Uncle Earl, this has been great, thank you. I think I've got it." He headed toward the door.

"The lesson ain't finished yet."

Levy turned around, stared at him.

"To really know what it's like to be a killer, you have to experience it yourself. And I got just the thing for you to do. See, my next door-neighbor, this pussy Warwick, is always coming around to my side of the lawn to pick his god-damn precious berries that grow over my fence. I've told him a hundred times not to do it, but he don't listen. I want you to go over and teach him a lesson."

Levy's eyes widened. "What?"

"Take the gun and go next door."

"I couldn't do that."

"It's the only way you're truly gonna learn how to be... what was that word you used? 'Authentic.'"

"I don't—"

"Relax. The gun won't have no bullets. I just want you to feel what it's like and maybe scare him a bit."

"I should go home."

Earl slowly walked over to Levy, grabbed his hand in a firm grip, almost breaking his fingers. "You asked for my help and I'm giving it to you."

Levy wanted to scream, but stifled himself. Earl let his hand go and looked at his watch.

"It's eleven, so that jerk's probably asleep right now. I want you to go into his bedroom—it's on the main floor. Got it?"

Levy realized he was stuck. He would have to go through with this. A few moments later, the two of them crept over to the next-door neighbor's back door. Earl, using a pick, opened the lock and sent Levy inside.

Levy crept through the dark house, stumbling over unexpected furniture a few times, but finally he heard snoring in one of the rooms.

He took a deep breath as he entered. He saw the form on the bed and tiptoed over. Then he pushed the gun barrel against Warwick's forehead and repeated the words he'd been told to say. "Get up, you bastard."

The craggy-faced man's eyes snapped open.

"Who the hell are you?"

"Your next-door neighbor sent me."

A look of horror filled Warwick's face. "That crazy."

"I said get up. This ain't no welcoming party." Levy added the last part, thinking it gave some panache to the line. "Earl doesn't want you coming over to his side of the yard to get your precious berries any more. Understand, you son of a bitch?"

Tears began flowing down the poor man's face. "Don't shoot. I won't do it again. I promise."

Levy felt some kind of pleasure making this man grovel. He wasn't *playing* a killer. He *was* one. Power filled his entire being, so much that he pulled the trigger.

A shot rang out.

The gun had bullets!

Warwick screamed as blood poured out of his chest.

It took a moment for Levy to realize just what he'd done. His heart pounded; he couldn't catch his breath. He dropped the gun and ran out of the house, shaking.

He raced down the street to the train station, looking back every minute to make sure no one was following him. Even on the train, his eyes kept darting from corner to corner. When he got home, he dashed inside, lay on his bed and covered himself up with blankets. He tried to sleep, but couldn't. He kept seeing Warwick's blood-drenched body. He figured Earl loaded bullets into the gun, thinking that Levy might just pull the trigger and get rid of the neighbor for him. It was the perfect crime. The police would never connect Earl to Warwick's death, because the gun had Levy's fingerprints all over it.

Would Earl tell the police what he'd done?

✗　✗　✗　✗

When morning came, Levy got out of bed, knowing what to do. He called Earl to remind him that he knew about the guy buried near Interstate 9.

"Actually, no one's buried there any more, kid. Sorry."

Levy felt all his hope dissolve. "I guess you plan on turning me in."

When Earl responded, his voice was gentle. "No way, kid. You're family. I'd never turn you in. I have the gun in my possession. No one will ever know about this… situation. Nothing to worry about. I have to say, though, I really appreciate what you did for me. But look, don't you have an audition or something?"

"I can't go now."

"Kid, this is what you dreamed of all your life. You gotta go. We'll talk."

Levy hung up and wasn't sure exactly how he felt. But he decided he'd go to the audition and think about everything else later on.

✗   ✗   ✗   ✗

When he walked into the audition hall, he noticed that instead of William Henry, a younger man with long black hair was sitting on a chair in front of the desk.

"Hi. I'm Jonathan Levy. I'm here to audition for—"

"Jonathan Levy? I've been waiting for you. You have the part."

Levy blinked, not understanding. "But I didn't audition again yet."

"I'm Mr. Henry's assistant. He said to make sure you were cast in the film."

Levy should have felt good, but something was wrong here. "Where's Mr. Henry?"

The man's eyes drooped and his mouth turned downward. "He, uh, got beat up and shot this morning."

Levy felt a pang of shock. "Who did it?"

The man shrugged. "Don't know, but just before he passed on, he told the nurse at the hospital to make sure his family was safe and that you got the part."

Levy didn't understand—until a moment later, when he received a text—"favor given, favor paid."

✗

Steve Shrott's short stories have appeared in 15 anthologies as well as numerous online and print magazines. He has written two humorous mystery novels (*Audition for Death* and *Dead Men Don't Get Married*) and a "how-to book" on comedy writing. Some of his jokes are in the Smithsonian Institution.

THE OCCURRENCE OF THE AIR APPARENT

AN AUGUSTUS ARGENT STORY

by Teel James Glenn

"Lord Croydon is most definitely dead," Dr. Augustus Argent said as he knelt beside our host's body. "Murdered!"

The group of party guests clustered in the doorway to His Lordship's study gasped as one at the statement.

"How can that be?" I called from the window where I had stuck my head out for a breath. The air of the room was foul. "The room was locked till I kicked the door in."

Indeed, after His Lordship was heard to cry for his daughter, a cry that was abruptly cut off, the servants pounded on the door, then summoned the party guests.

I'd shouldered into the room to find it thick with gas from the extinguished sconces and had gone straight to the window to unlock and open it.

"There can be no doubt of the nature of his death, Jack," Dr. Argent said to me. "He has been strangled!" He pointed and by the light that streamed in from the full moon and from the inner door, I could see the true state of the dead man. The mustachioed lord's face was horribly distorted in fear, his tongue protruding and swollen, his eyes bulging. The most telling thing, however, were the clear marks of bruising around his neck that resembled the imprint of fingers!

"Father!" His Lordship's daughter Jean, a pretty blond girl, exclaimed as she pushed her way into the room. Her husband was forced to restrain her.

Dr. Argent rose and said, "There is nothing more to be done here, Jack. I think the room is sufficiently aerated. Let us relight the lamps, then close the door to preserve things for Scotland Yard."

I did as he requested, left the window of the second-floor room open and stepped out into the hall with him.

The other party guests and some servants stood around uncomfortably.

Dr. Augustus Argent was my friend and employer, but even if he were not, he would have commanded my attention as he did that of the dozen gathered individuals.

He stood over six feet and was lean and catlike in his movements, with long delicate fingers and eyes that sparkled with both wit and intelligence.

He wore his silver hair long and had a mustache and goatee, so that he resembled nothing so much as an American frontier figure, though his speech and manners were of the most British variety.

"I suggest we all retire to the ballroom," my mentor said to the crowd, "and await the authorities." He designated two servants to stand guard at the door, but then said quietly to me, "Jack, you know my methods and have a keen eye; make a thorough examination of the room and report to me."

I waited till he shepherded the others away, then reentered the murder room, pulling the shattered door closed behind me.

The study was in every way the typical sanctum for a man of Lord Croydon's position and interests as an eminent archeologist and member of the House of Lords. It was mostly dark wood, the bookshelves lining the walls containing one of the great collections on the study of antiquity.

Everywhere were souvenirs of His Lordship's many digs through the Middle East—African masks, a *kindjal*, a scarab necklace, an exotic and exquisite Persian silk painting of Aladdin—all casually arrayed amongst the technological creations His Lordship was famous for—special lamps created to work in dark caves, an electrically powered pump to drain water from sunken digs, and various miniature models of steam shovels and other earth-moving devices.

The nobleman could sit at his desk while he worked and look up to be reminded of his journeys and accomplishments in one sweeping glance.

He would never do that again, of course, for he was stretched out before his desk on the floor.

Lord Croydon had been in his late sixties, though from all reports vital, having just returned from his latest expedition to Arabia. He had a fringe of white hair and a full beard. He had been distinguished and even once handsome, but his features were so distorted by the manner of his death that they were hard to look at. In his right hand he held a jeweled broach unlike any other I had ever seen.

I tore my eyes from the gruesome sight to make a detailed survey of the room for Dr. Argent.

I went to the window again and reexamined the latch that had been firmly fastened when I opened it. There were no marks of tampering, no sign of a string or other means by which it could have been refastened from the outside if the killer exited that way.

"Secure," I said aloud, as if to assure myself.

I leaned out to look at the ground beneath the window for any further evidence, but the moonlight clearly showed no telltale marks of a ladder nor footprints.

Next, I craned my neck to look up at the eaves, but the ivy was undisturbed, and the overhang clearly offered no purchase.

With that avenue of escape eliminated, I examined the room's interior in detail. I sounded out every inch of the walls and floors for any hidden exits, trap doors, or escape stairs.

There were none, save the small wall safe hidden behind a false set of books on a top shelf. The safe was unopened as far as I could determine.

My last act was to minutely examine the now-broken lock of the door. It had been intact before my brute entrance and showed no other signs of being picked, the key still on the interior.

I left as baffled as when I entered the room.

Downstairs, Dr. Argent had gathered all the guests and servants, save the two on guard by the study, in the ballroom where they were surrounded by trinkets of long dead caliphs.

The large window-lined room had been turned into an exhibit hall to showcase the artifacts from Lord Croydon's dig on the Arabian peninsula. Tables were strewn with lamps, daggers, plaques, urns and such other treasures that he recovered, each polished and labeled for examination before he donated them to the Royal Museum.

"Ladies and gentlemen," the Guv (as I call Dr. Argent) said, "I pray your patience as we await authorities to investigate fully."

I knew he was being less than fully truthful with the guests as his position as Minister Without Portfolio for Occult Affairs allowed him full latitude to act in the matter of His Lordship's murder.

I am Jack Stone and was seconded to Dr. Argent from the Horseguard, to serve as his assistant after I became aware of his fighting the shadow war on behalf of the Empire.

"Why?" Jean Pertwee, His Lordship's daughter sobbed. "Father had just gone up to his study to get a jeweled broach from his safe that he'd forgotten for the exhibit."

"Easy, dear," her husband Jason said, patting her arm. He offered her a sherry and glared at Dr. Argent. He was a robust fellow with dark brown hair and regular features. His eyes were shards of yellow diamonds that he fixed on the Guv.

"What can be done, Dr. Argent?" Pertwee demanded. "Something must be done!"

"What can be done will be done," my silver haired mentor said. "First we must establish the whereabouts of everyone here—"

"But we were all in this room," said Adam Kinter, Lord Croydon's assistant on archeological digs. He wore thick glasses and affected a cane for style.

"We will determine exactly where everyone was in due time," Dr. Argent said. "We must gather all the facts. If each of you would recount your whereabouts when you heard the shout that caused you to rush to His Lordship's study."

Each guest and servant then recounted their exact position when the butler Collins proclaimed that he heard His Lordship cry out his daughter's name.

Each guest or servant was vouched for and verified by at least one other.

Adam Kinter had been observed the entire time at the far end of the ballroom, bent over one of the exhibits, polishing it and talking quietly to himself.

Jean, the daughter, was among a group of women, chatting excitedly and looking for her husband, who could not be located.

"I'd stepped outside for a cigar," the burly Jason Pertwee said curtly. "Jean doesn't like the smell."

"I don't like the smell of that." Adam Kinter inserted himself. "What was he *really* doing?"

"Kinter," Pertwee replied. "Ever since Jean chose me over you, you've—"

"Sir!" Dr. Argent said with a finality that made all turn toward him. "You will only upset Lady Jean further—and complicate our difficulties; your whereabouts matter, as you are the only one unaccounted for at the time of His Lordship's death."

"I don't have to explain myself to anyone, least of all you," Pertwee objected.

"Actually, sirrah, you do," I spoke up, not willing to brook such impertinence to my employer. "Dr. Argent is empowered by the Crown to—"

I caught a look somewhere between amusement and caution from the Guv that caused me to pause.

Adam Kinter used that opportunity to interject, "Ask Jason who had the most to gain by His Lordship's death."

"Adam!" Jean Pertwee cried, "How could you? Are you so upset that my father discharged you for continuing to bother me? He let you come to this unveiling because you helped on the dig, but—"

"Jason took you," Kinter protested. "He wormed his way onto the Arabian dig and your father's confidence, then tricked you into marrying him so he would be His Lordship's heir!"

"You bounder!" Jason Pertwee stepped forward, only to be restrained by his wife.

"Enough!" Dr. Argent said with a tone that halted all and caused all eyes to turn toward him. He held us transfixed for a long second, his keen eyes taking the whole room. Then he said with a nod of his head, "I know what happened to His Lordship and want only for a single proof to apprehend the villain."

There was a collective gasp from all present, including myself.

"What happened to my father?" Jean asked in a child-like voice. "Who—?"

"I am afraid, Mrs. Pertwee," the Guv said, "I am not prepared to voice my postulations quite yet."

He turned to me. "First, Jack, we must return to the site of the murder to conduct an experiment; I am sure we will then be able to tell these good people who the killer is."

He then addressed the room. "You must all stay in sight of each other while we are gone. When we return, we shall proclaim the name of the murderer to you all."

I obediently followed the silver-haired minister up to the study where he dismissed the servants, then closed the door and pushed a heavy chair against it.

The death scene was eerie in the waning moonlight, the ancient artifacts and modern machinery a strange backdrop for the horror of His Lordship's mortal remains.

I turned up the gas lamps and asked, "What next, Doctor?"

My employer gave a short laugh and said, "We wait for the killer to strike us down."

"Sir?"

The Doctor seemed to ignore my question and moved to examine one of the devices on a wooden stand near the wall. It was a thing of tubes and hose, with a large clear vessel like an inverted punchbowl, or deep-sea diver's helmet.

"Lord Croydon was an inventive genius," Dr. Argent said. "According to his notes, this is a proto-type pump to extract seepage in digs. The liquid goes into this reservoir to be visually examined before being filtered, and sediment of various sizes is let out through this end." He reached over to twist a valve. "Now it is closed, so it will not empty."

He turned a dial and the electrical batteries connected to the device began to hum.

"Well and good," I said, confused by his lecture, "but what has this to do with the killer of which you spoke? We have to stop him."

"We shall, Jack," the Guv said. "As soon as he comes to kill us."

Before I could respond, the scones began to flicker and then one of the gas lamps flared up brightly as all the others went out. The flame on the single jet grew blue, its aspect becoming smoky. This smoke poured from the sconce to spill to the floor till it resembled nothing so much as a miniature version of the Pillar of Smoke and Fire, such as Moses must have followed.

"Ah, Jack," Dr. Argent said in reaction to my surprise at the apparition. "It is as I thought; be prepared to turn that switch when

I say." He pointed to the siphoning device, then picked up a length of tubing connected to it and turned to face the pillar.

The smoky column resolved itself into a shape like that of a tall, strongly-built man, though with distinctly blue-tinted skin and sharp facial features that include high cheekbones and a hooked nose.

This new arrival was naked and very much a perfect male figure in every way, save that he had cloven hooves where feet should be.

"*As-salaam 'alaykum,*" Dr. Argent said.

"*Masaa' al-khayr,*" The blue man replied in a deep voice. His figure wavered in the pale moonlight that now illuminated the room, as if he were still composed of smoke.

"You know why I am here, *effendi*?" the man asked.

"Yes," Dr. Argent said. "Your master has dispatched you to end our lives, because he is afraid I have discovered him."

"Just so," the blue man said. "I bear no malice but must do as bidden."

"As well all must," my mentor said. He added, "Now, Jack!"

I threw the switch.

The vacuum machine turned on with a whining sound.

Dr. Argent pointed the tube at the blue man and in an instant the apparition became distorted and, like real smoke, was drawn into the pump device.

In an instant the blue smoke was swirling in the glass bowl, filling the reservoir. Dr. Argent reached over to turn off the machine and the valves closed the entrance and exit of the reservoir to effectively trap the blue smoke.

"You should relight the lamps, Jack," Dr. Argent said. "We are quite safe now. This fellow's master is a coward and will do nothing even when he discovers his 'assassin' has failed."

I did as he asked. When I turned back he was crouched down to peer into the blue mist that filled the globe.

The odd thing was that the features of the blue-faced man were still clearly visible in the mist, albeit distorted, floating in the glass bowl. What was remarkable was that the misty face gazed back at my mentor with hooded eyes, apparently resigned to his fate.

"Almost done, Jack," Dr. Argent said. "All that is left is to arrest the one who sent this fellow to do us mischief."

"But— But—" I asked. "What have I just witnessed? Who— or what is this fellow?"

"The Quran says that he and his kind are made of a smokeless and scorching fire, but are also physical in nature, being able to interact in a tactile manner with people and objects, and likewise be acted upon. Neither good nor evil, but servant to any who command them."

"What— what is he?" I asked.

"He is what the Lord recognized him to be, Jack. You see, the butler heard incorrectly when His Lordship called out in his last desperate moments; he was not calling out his daughter's name, he was naming the instrument of his death: a Jinn!"

"A genie?" I gasped. "But who summoned him?"

Dr. Argent gave a cold smile. "The only person who knew that the enchanted lamp needed to be rubbed, who appeared to be mumbling to himself when, in fact, he was giving orders to the Jinn within that lamp."

"Kinter?"

"Yes," Dr. Argent said. "The spurned lover who got his revenge on his employer and did his best to cast the shadow of guilt on his rival, perhaps in hopes of regaining his lost lady's love. Let us go downstairs and make the arrest."

"What about— him?" I pointed to the glass globe where the blue Jinn was eyeing us with a perturbed expression.

"Ah, well," the Guv said. "He will be here when we get back with his lamp to counteract his last order and give him new ones. I fancy we could use a new coach that has better springs than the one Her Majesty provided for us before we send him on his way!"

✗

Teel James Glenn's stories have been printed in magazines from *Weird Tales*, *Spinetingler*, *SciFan*, *Mad*, *Black Belt*, *Fantasy Tales*, *Crimson Streets*, *Silver Blade Quarterly*, *Blazing Adventures*, and scores of other publications. He is also the winner of the 2012 Pulp Ark Award for Best Author. His website is: theurbanswashbuckler.com

RETRIBUTION

by Peter James Quirk

As I approach my exit, I glance into my rear-view mirror and ease over into the empty right-hand lane. Moments later a police cruiser, lights flashing and siren blasting, is riding my rear bumper. At first I think he simply wishes to pass, so I pull onto the shoulder, but to my dismay, he pulls in right behind me. I sit bemused and silent as I watch a lily-white deputy climb out of his vehicle, adjust his Smokey-bear campaign hat, push out his barrel chest and approach my driver's-side window.

"License and registration," he says testily.

Oh my, I think, a cop in a bad mood. How did I get so lucky? Nonetheless, I reply politely, employing Ivy-league enunciation. "Good evening, Officer. What seems to be the problem?"

"The problem is that I want your license and registration and you're sitting there asking stupid questions."

"But why on earth did you pull me over? I did nothing wrong."

"When an officer of the law gives someone like you a directive, it's up to you to comply. Hand me your license and registration and don't make any abrupt or suspicious moves."

If I believe at first this situation is preposterous or even mildly funny, I soon realize that if I'm not very careful, I'm going to be arrested or even shot—much like the two young black men whose shooting by police in Fairhaven two nights ago I'm on my way to investigate.

✗   ✗   ✗   ✗

Salina Robbins is my name and I'm a black journalist with feminist leanings writing for the *Wessex Gazette*, a newspaper covering a county of predominately middle-class white republicans. And while most of my assignments are routine or even boring, for once I'm pursuing an event of state-wide, even national import:

Two nights ago, a white middle-aged woman living alone in Fairhaven, a suburban community fifteen miles north of the

Borough of Wessex, calls 9-1-1 to report that two men are attempting to break into her house. And fifteen minutes later, the suspects—black men—are shot dead by the responding police on the sidewalk. One of the young men is a former Wessex High School football star named LeRoy Alberts and my editor believes that might provide an additional twist to the drama.

The first thing I do upon receiving the assignment is to telephone Betsy Alberts, LeRoy's mother, but when there is no answer I try Miriam Harris, the woman who originally called in the 9-1-1: "Ms. Harris? This is Salina Robbins from the *Wessex Gazette*. May I have a moment of your time for a short interview?"

"I don't know; I'm kind of busy. I have to go shopping for my father."

"Oh, I'm sorry, is he sick?"

"No, he's old and deaf. He lives across the street and I take care of him."

"Well, perhaps I could stop by this evening; would that be okay?"

"If you could come around eight-thirty—by that time I will have fed him and put him to bed."

"We should all have a daughter like you in our declining years, Ms. Harris. I'll see you at eight-thirty, then."

And after getting directions to Ms. Harris's house, I try LeRoy Alberts's mother again. This time the phone picks up: "Mrs. Alberts? This is Salina Robbins from the *Wessex Gazette*, and I'm sorry to bother you at such a difficult time, but I'd like to have a word with you if I may. Would that be possible?"

"This is a household in mourning, Ms. Robbins. We're not answering questions at this time. Please address any and all enquiries to Reginald B. Armstrong, Esquire, Attorney-at-law. Thank you for your interest." And after reading that coached response in a slow monotone, Mrs. Alberts hangs up.

I do not know Reginald Armstrong personally, but I know his background. His father was a respected civil rights leader who marched with Martin Luther King, Jr. And although Armstrong maintains an office in Wessex, he made his reputation with several cases of suspected police abuse of young black men and their rights in county communities with much larger minority populations. Apparently my editor's instincts were right on target, because although Armstrong is not a headlines chaser, he has a reputation as a strong civil-rights advocate who works quietly and efficiently behind the scenes to get justice for his clients. I call his office and make an appointment for an interview.

✗   ✗   ✗   ✗

And that evening I pull up outside Miriam Harris's house. I'm in a foul mood after my encounter with Smokey-the-Bear, and my ticket for driving while black sits on my dashboard rubbing salt into the wounds of my self-respect. I shake it off by reminding myself I have a job to do and ring Mrs. Harris's front-door bell.

"Mrs. Harris? Salina Robbins from the *Gazette*; we spoke earlier. I'll try not to take up too much of your time. I trust your father is well?"

"Hello, please come in and thanks for asking. He's as well as can be expected for a man of his age. Sit over there, Ms. Robbins. Can I get you anything—something to drink perhaps, a cup of tea?"

"Please call me Salina, but I wouldn't want to put you to any trouble...."

"It's no trouble at all. I grew up in an English household where the tea kettle was always on the stove. And call me Miriam."

"Then a cup of tea would be nice," I said, not wishing to offend my interviewee. And as soon as the tea is served I ask her to tell me exactly what happened on the night of the 22nd.

"Well, I heard noises outside. First someone was pulling on the garage door, but when I saw two men sneaking around out back, I panicked and called 9-1-1. Then I switched out all the lights and hid in my bedroom closet."

"Did you notice what color they were, Miriam?"

"No, I really didn't think about that. This is a white neighborhood and usually any trouble-making or break-ins are white teenage boys who've been out boozing or doing drugs."

"So then what happened?"

"Well, I heard gunshots and then a little while later, my cell phone rang: It was the police telling me that the intruders had been subdued and that they would like to come in and search the house. I didn't learn until the following day they were dead."

When the interview is over, Ms. Harris shows me out, but as I leave I turn to ask a final question. "One more thing, Miriam. How did your father react to all this commotion?" I turn and look up and down the road. "Which is his house, anyway?"

Miriam waves her arm vaguely across the road towards a house to the left. "He didn't hear anything," she said. "As I told you, he's pretty deaf. Have a good evening." And with that she quickly closes her door.

After I return to my car, I sit staring at Miriam's father's house for a few moments before I start my engine. Why doesn't she want me to talk with him? Could it be he's bigoted, too? Or is that simply paranoia emanating from my confrontation with Smokey? But even those ugly thoughts fade as I begin thinking of the questions I will put to Reginald Armstrong, Esquire.

✗ ✗ ✗ ✗

"Good morning, Ms. Robbins, please take a seat. I'm surprised we've never met before. I thought I knew most local journalists—I've met your editor on several occasions. He never mentioned he had someone as pretty as you on his staff." Reginald Armstrong smiles warmly, showing a mouth full of strong white teeth and holds out his hand.

"You're a fine looking man yourself, Mr. Armstrong, mighty fine," I say, laying on a little street. "But I didn't come here looking for a hook-up. Shall we get down to business? Two young black men are dead and you are representing the Alberts family. Why did Mrs. Alberts feel the need to engage you?"

"She called initially because nobody would allow her to view her son's body. I managed to get around the red tape for her and accompanied her to the morgue. And I'm glad I did, because prior to being shot, both men were badly beaten about the head and body."

"Really?" I say. "They were beaten with what, exactly?"

"Nobody knows. The police are not admitting to any improper behavior. They say they are waiting for an autopsy report, which I understand will be issued by the end of the week."

"So, counselor, what do you think happened?"

"Quite frankly, they looked to me as though they'd been in a bar fight, which didn't make much sense."

"Did any cops get treated for injuries at the hospital, I wonder?"

"I couldn't say, but the suspects could have been beaten at gun point."

"Perhaps I should talk to some neighbors. They may have seen or heard something. I'll do that and also check the hospital for police injuries. There's not much else we can do right now. Do you know which police department answered the 9-1-1 call?"

"It was the County Sheriff's department. Fairhaven doesn't have its own police force."

"I might have known. I had a run in with one of their deputies yesterday. He was very unfriendly and I received a totally unnecessary ticket for changing lanes without using directional signals. Do you know the Sheriff? What is he like?"

"I've met him. His name is Olaf Pettersen and he has a reputation for being unsympathetic to minorities. But if his men did what it seems they did, someone's going to have a field day with him and his department in court. But until the autopsy results are made known, this is all speculation. Tell me, Ms. Robbins, are you a local girl?"

"My mother was born in Wessex Borough and I lived here as a child. And when I graduated from Dartmouth, I moved back because I always enjoyed the integrated cultural scene. Unfortunately, that scene doesn't seem to extend beyond the borough limits."

"Do you have a degree in journalism?"

"No, it's actually in creative writing. This job is simply to keep me solvent until I write the great American novel."

"Don't you mean the great Black-American novel?"

"To tell you the truth, I was mostly sheltered from the black/white cultural divide growing up and in college. I'm actually more involved with women's rights. My encounter with Smokey the Bear was a real eye-opener."

"I assume that means that you haven't begun the writing yet?"

"But at least now I'm thinking about it. That's a start, wouldn't you say?"

"If we have to try this case and we win it, Ms. Robbins, perhaps I might assist you with your solvency problem by taking you out to dinner?"

"Perhaps, Mr. Armstrong; I'm sure you would be a wealth of information for someone writing *Invisible Woman*."

Armstrong smiled at the Ellison reference. "If you had been invisible yesterday, you wouldn't have got that ticket. By the way, please call me Reggie."

"And I'm Salina, but you're quite correct. That title won't do at all. It will have to be much more relevant than that."

⨰   ⨰   ⨰   ⨰

The next morning I am back in Fairhaven to interview Miriam Harris's neighbors. I park a few doors down from her house, go through my questions and wonder where to begin when, just as I am about to step onto the sidewalk, Miriam's father's garage door opens and a vintage army jeep backs out and on to the road. And as I sit and watch, the jeep drives right by me and turns at the end of the road toward the business district. I am very surprised by what I see.

The driver, certainly an elderly gentleman, is alone in the car, but that's not what surprises me. His face is creased with age, of course, but he has a strong jaw and a flat boxer's nose and he's wearing a baseball cap turned backward over long wavy salt-and-pepper hair. I can only see his arms and shoulders, but he is wearing a black sleeveless tee shirt and the tattooed arms that grasp the steering wheel are bulging with muscles. This is no frail old guy; I am looking at a retired version of Popeye the sailor man. Instinctively I start up my car and pull out behind him.

The jeep drives three blocks over to a lake front and pulls into a coffee shop parking lot. I park my car and watch as he strides toward the door. He is average height, but he is straight backed, upright and shows no sign of infirmity. I wait in the parking lot long enough to realize he is not simply buying a coffee to go and then I lock up my car and follow him inside.

Popeye is sitting at the diner counter bantering with a buxom blond waitress who is probably on the wrong side of forty, but not much older. She addresses him fondly as Charlie or darling and it is apparent they know each other well. I sit at the other end of the counter.

"I'm glad you sat all the way down here," says the blonde, whose name tag labels her as LaRae. "This is how I get my exercise."

"Oh, I'm sorry, would you like me to move down to the other end?"

"If you don't mind, but only if you don't make any moves on Charlie. He belongs to me."

I glance down the counter to where Popeye is beaming at both of us. "Don't you listen to LaRae, my love," he says with an ebullient Cockney accent. "I'm big and strong enough for both of you." I chuckle and move on down beside him.

"I'm Salina and I'm happy to make your acquaintance. May I call you Charlie?"

"Everyone else does, darling. Can I buy you breakfast?"

I am surprised by that remark, but I am also beginning to enjoy myself. Charlie's irrepressible spirit is contagious. "I'd better buy my own," I say. "We wouldn't want to make LaRae jealous, now would we?"

LaRae winks at Charlie and smiles at me as she takes my order. But Charlie is outraged. "That's all you're going to eat, Salina, an English muffin? You won't get far on that."

"I'm sure you've heard that saying about girlish figures, Charlie. Well, it may be a cliché, but it's true enough. Frankly, I'm surprised at the huge breakfast you're eating. Where do you put it all? You don't have an ounce of fat on you anywhere."

"When I leave here I'm off to the gym for a couple of hours and when I'm done I walk around the lake before I go home. I used to run, but I hurt my knee a couple of years ago."

"I've been meaning to go to a gym, but I never get around to it. Where is yours?"

"It's Planet Fitness; it's out on the highway about two miles from here."

"That's too far for me. I live in Wessex."

"That's too bad, Salina, because I could take you as my guest, show you around the machines and teach you how to use them."

"Now that's an offer I couldn't possibly refuse. How about I take you up on that tomorrow? I could meet you here and buy you breakfast. How's nine-thirty?"

"Nine-thirty would be great," says Charlie. "I'm looking forward to it already."

"Don't do anything I wouldn't do," says LaRae as she hands Charlie his check. She turns to me: "He's eighty-four years old, you know."

I simply shake my head in wonder as I slide off my stool. "I'll see you tomorrow, Charlie."

⚹   ⚹   ⚹   ⚹

My next stop is the emergency room, which confirms no deputies were treated for wounds on the evening of October 22nd. I then return to the *Gazette* building, where I call the coroner's office to see if their Autopsy report is released—it is, so I head to the County Sheriff's department HQ on Wessex Avenue.

I give my card to the receptionist and ask to speak to Sheriff Pettersen. She calls my name in to his office. "He says he will give you ten minutes. Please show yourself in."

The sheriff—a tall Norwegian who is now middle-aged and paunchy—stands as I walk in, although there is no visible sign that I am welcome. "What can I do for you?" he asks in a matter-of-fact tone after he points to a seat.

I explain who I am again, what I am working on and ask if he has seen the autopsy report on LeRoy Walters and Michael Ellis. He nods. "I've just read it. They died of gunshot wounds. There was nothing surprising there at all."

"But was it necessary to shoot them? Couldn't you have simply arrested them and taken them into custody?"

"I don't have to explain the actions of my department to the likes of you," he says, "but they were attempting to break away, and if they do not obey a police command to stop running, my men are trained to do whatever is necessary to prevent that."

"But what about their other injuries—their black eyes, one had a broken nose, the other a broken jaw?"

"My officers all swear that nobody laid a hand on them and that any injuries they may have sustained were pre-existing. I have no reason to doubt their word and will back them to the hilt in any court of law."

"Well, good luck with that, Sheriff. I hear the Alberts family is preparing a lawsuit."

"I have nothing more to say on the subject. Good day to you, Ms. Robbins."

✗   ✗   ✗   ✗

The next day I arrive early at the Lake Coffee House in Fairhaven. I have some questions for LaRae. "Hi, honey," she says. "Charlie's not here yet."

"That's okay, LaRae. I'd like to ask you about him before he gets here. Do you know his daughter Miriam?"

"Oh, yeah, she comes in with him once in a while. Why? Do you know her, too?"

I explain how we met and add, "Why is she so protective of him? Charlie seems like a guy who could look after himself very well."

"Apparently Charlie is severely dyslexic, plus he was a pro boxer for about ten years. So between the dyslexia and being constantly punched in the head, he has trouble reading, writing, and paying his bills. He can be hard of hearing, too. Of course that wasn't so much of a problem when his wife was alive. But she passed away last year, and Miriam moved back to the area to be close to him. Here's Charlie now; don't say a word about this. Miriam told me he's very self-conscious about his reading problems."

"Hello, girls, you're not fighting over me, are you?" Charlie kisses me on the cheek and swings himself up onto the next stool, grinning from ear to ear.

"No, Charlie, we've decided to share you. We were just working out a schedule."

I ride to Planet Fitness in Charlie's jeep and I spend the next two hours watching him work the weight machines and getting to know as much about him as I possibly can. He has lived a hard life: after surviving the London Blitz and the East End street gangs, he takes up boxing after a few months in prison for knocking cold a policeman and has a pretty successful ten-year career. He then comes to America with his family and makes a living nailing on roof shingles in both the hot summer sun and the cold snowy winter. This is one tough old dude!

I soon get an idea what really happens outside his daughter's house, although I don't actually ask Charlie anything until we have been working out together for a week. By this time the story is national news, especially as the Wessex County District Attorney has reviewed the case and decided not to prosecute the two deputies responsible for the shootings. There is a public outcry swelling in the Wessex Borough black community and outrage is spreading across the state.

Meanwhile, I hear from LaRae that Charlie has a birthday coming up. And I take him to a sports bar to watch a fight. "So, Charlie," I say, when we are deep into our third beer, "what really happened that night at Miriam's?"

✗   ✗   ✗   ✗

I am present in court on the first day of the Alberts family suit against the Wessex County Sheriff's Department and I find myself holding my breath in anticipation as Reginald Armstrong, counsel for the plaintiff, rises to address his opening remarks to the jury: "Good morning, ladies and gentlemen. I am here today on behalf of the Alberts family, who are seeking justice for the life of LeRoy Alberts, a recent high school football star and a young life cut cruelly short in its prime." Reggie pauses as he scans the faces of the jury members, no doubt looking for signs of empathy.

"By pressing this suit, the Alberts family is not suggesting that LeRoy was a saint, but he was young and full of energy and they are sure he would have turned his life around given the opportunity. Unfortunately this opportunity was taken away by the hasty and unthinking actions of the authorities. The Sheriff's department, however, maintains that LeRoy was attempting to escape, even as they try to explain away his injuries, which suggest a thorough beating, from which he would have had a difficult time running anywhere." Reggie pauses again, this time for effect, and ends his remarks by saying that he has complete faith in the jury's ability to come to a just verdict and award the Alberts family ample compensation for their terrible loss.

When the opening remarks are complete, Judge Reynolds asks Counselor Armstrong to call his first witness. "I call Mr. Charles Harris to the stand," says Reggie as he turns and smiles briefly in my direction.

Charlie steps into the courtroom erect and proud in a new charcoal suit, a crisp white shirt and solid blue tie—an outfit I pick out for him personally. His long wavy hair is freshly cut and combed. And I am sitting there beaming as he walks past me, proud and erect, on his way to the witness stand.

"Do your thing, Charlie darling," I say to myself.

After Charlie is sworn in, Counselor Armstrong asks him enough questions to establish his identity and then as a mood of quiet expectation descends on the courtroom, he asks him to relate in his own words the events of the evening of October 22nd.

"Well, my daughter called me to say there were two men trying to break into her house…"

"Would you please establish for the court who exactly is your daughter, Mr. Harris?"

"Miriam Harris, of course," says Charlie, looking mildly annoyed.

"And she is the owner of the house?"

"You know that as well as I do."

"My apologies, Mr. Harris. We are merely establishing the facts for the jury's consideration."

Charlie, however, still seems annoyed.

"And at what time did she call?"

"I don't know, do I? But she said she was going to call 9-1-1, too, and you must have a record of that."

"I'm sure we do, Mr. Harris. So then what happened?"

"So I go running over there, don't I, and these two black blokes skulking in the shadows don't say a word—they just jump me."

"Wait a minute, Mr. Harris. You look in remarkably good health for an elderly man who was recently mugged by suspected felons. There is no sign of any injury at all on your face or body."

"I said they jumped me; I didn't say they were any good at it."

At that moment the entire courtroom erupts into laughter and Judge Reynolds, who has to work at fighting back his own smiles, raps his gavel on the desk. "Silence in the court," he says. And when the laughter subsides, he motions to Charlie to continue.

"I put them away in no time, Your Honor; left hook, right cross, one two, one two, and then I put in the boot—piece of cake. Then Miriam comes to the door and tells me the police are on their way. So I ask her what she thinks I should do. She tells me to go back home and not to answer the door and she would take care of the police and try to keep me out of it. I trust her, so I did exactly that and the moment I closed my front door, I heard police cars come screaming around the corner. And that's all I know."

"Mr. Harris, would you please explain to the court exactly what you mean when you say you put in the boot?"

"I was wearing construction boots and before I left I kicked them both in the knee. They weren't going anywhere after that."

"So, Mr. Harris, you are telling the court that just moments before the police arrived, both suspects were incapacitated, even unconscious. Is that correct?"

"I believe so," says Charlie.

"And they would have had a great deal of difficulty getting away from them?"

"A referee could have counted to a hundred and fifty and they still would have been out—unless I've lost my touch." Charlie grinned at the judge.

"That's all the questions I have for this witness, Your Honor," says Reggie.

Judge Reynolds nods and turns to Jonathan Rodgers, the counsel for the Sheriff's department. "Do you wish to cross-examine this witness, Counselor?"

"In the light of this evidence, I should like the time to confer with my clients before continuing, Your Honor."

"I'm sure you would, Counselor." Judge Reynolds glances at the wall clock and then bangs down his gavel. "This court will reconvene tomorrow morning at ten o'clock."

✗   ✗   ✗   ✗

A few weeks after the excitement of the civil trial in which both deputies are found guilty of willfully violating their prisoners's civil rights and the Alberts family is awarded five million dollars in compensation, I experience a spiritual let-down. Both Reggie and Charlie become media stars in their own right, although Charlie soon gets tired of dressing up for the morning news shows and longs to escape back to his former uncomplicated life. Reggie, on the other hand, is happily promoting his racial agenda—I see him on Sunday morning news shows regularly. But even he finally takes the time to pick up the phone.

"Have you started writing *Invisible Woman* yet?" he says, as though he has been calling me every day.

"Where the hell have you been?" I counter, sounding much too much like an aggrieved spouse.

"I've been on the media roundabout and couldn't jump off."

"Couldn't or wouldn't?"

"Does it really matter? I did what I had to do, but I'm back in Wessex now and I thought I would give you a call. How's Charlie?"

"He's hiding out. The last time I talked to him, he told me he's had an offer of $50,000 from a publishing house for a memoir and someone else wants him to make a fitness video for seniors. But he says he's tired of the spotlight—he's turned them both down."

"You should write the memoir for him, Salina. It would give you the discipline you need to write your own book."

"This is the first time I've heard from you in weeks and you're already harassing me about my work ethic? What's it got to do with you, anyway?"

"I like the thought of having a successful writer for a girlfriend."

"Now I'm your girlfriend?" I say, my voice rising in crescendo. "In your dreams, Counselor."

"Be nice, Salina. I was calling to invite you to our long-delayed dinner date. What do you say?"

✗

Peter James Quirk is an author, freelance writer and outdoorsman who spends his winters skiing and snowboarding and his summers hiking, biking, and playing tennis. His novel *Trail of Vengeance* has a strong ski theme; indeed, the villain of the story is a disgraced ski instructor. Many of his stories, however, cover World War II and its aftermath. It is a fascinating, if tragic, period to explore, and the villains and heroes are so easy to find.

MURDER AT A MILITARY FUNERAL

by Archie Goodwin

TRANSCRIBED BY MARVIN KAYE

I told Nero Wolfe, "I've got to go to Florida."

"Why?"

"My Uncle Joe died. He was an army sergeant and was wounded in action, so it'll be a military funeral, complete with twenty-one gun salute."

He put his bookmark in Kate Caffrey's book about *The Mayflower* and said, "Isn't that unusual for a sergeant?"

"I thought so, too, at first, but my aunt wanted it and it turns out that any veteran can have the ceremony if you ask the American Legion."

"Interesting. So how long will you be gone?"

"Only a day, I think. Tomorrow, and I'll be back Monday."

"Good." He returned his attention to his book and I went upstairs to pack.

✗   ✗   ✗   ✗

I met my Aunt Edith in a cemetery near Tampa. She pointed out the seven men standing by with their rifles and said they were an honour guard sent by the American Legion.

"I'm glad you could come, Archie."

"Well, you know you were always my favorite aunt and uncle."

She smiled through her black veil. "He thought of you practically as a son."

"I loved going on sales trips with him." My uncle was a crack salesman for Tru-Sewn Slippers.

"I think," she said, "they're ready to begin."

We approached the coffin. It was a balmy day just before noon and not counting the honour guard, there were five others in attendance besides us. One well-dressed chap of about seventy stood near us to the right while a little way off on our left there were four other men, all of them at least sixty, probably older. I asked who they all were.

"The man near us is Sam Marker, the owner of Tru-Sewn Slippers. Your uncle worked for him. I'm not sure who the others are, though a couple of them look familiar."

The ceremony began. A white-haired minister who I later learned was a retired military chaplain gave a brief summary of "the life of Sergeant Joseph C. Parkus. He lived a good life and was loved by all who knew him. I'm told that some years before he enlisted he was on the vaudeville circuit as a one-man band."

That jogged my memory. He once gave me a set of drumsticks and a few lessons in how to hold them and play on a snare drum, which he also gave me. In my room I had two black, slightly-curved sticks called bones, which he also showed me how to use. Yes, he was a fun uncle.

The chaplain said, "Is there anyone here who'd like to say a few words about Sergeant Parkus?"

Sam Marker stepped forward. "Joey was not only my best salesman, he was popular everywhere he traveled. He didn't just know how to talk, but how to listen… and he also knew many very funny jokes, most of which we could never tell here." That made a couple of the old men on our left chuckle. "I thought of him as a personal friend." With that he returned to his place near us.

I took his place and talked about some of the sales trips he took me on. "They were lots of fun," I reminisced. "At night there was always a great meal to look forward to with a movie afterward. I remember him taking me to dinner at the Hotel Bethlehem in Pennsylvania—which is pretty far away from his sales territory, but he never minded a long drive for good food. Anyway, when we were done the waiter brought us bowls of warm water with rose petals in them. I didn't know what they were for, so my uncle explained the mysteries of the finger-bowl." I sighed. "I'm really going to miss him."

I walked back to Aunt E (as she prefers to be called) and the chaplain said a few more words, this time from the Bible and that ended the ceremony.

The seven riflemen stepped forward and fired three volleys.

With a cry, Sam Marker fell down. I went over to him, saw the bullet-hole in his chest, checked his breath and pulse, then told the chaplain that he was dead. To everyone else I said, "Nobody move. We've got to wait for the police."

✗ ✗ ✗ ✗

The cops didn't take long to show up. With them was Inspector Yaeger, a sour-looking stump who chewed on an unlit cigar, which naturally made me think of our old friend Cramer.

The inspector spoke with the chaplain and then the riflemen. Aunt E and I were next.

"The way I see it," he said, "I've got six suspects."

"Six?" my aunt repeated. "All right, of course you're discounting the chaplain, but what about the honour guard?"

"Naah. They all fired into the air. I did ask them if one of them might have aimed at Marker, instead, but they told me that anyone who did that would definitely be seen by one or more of them. So like I said, six, though I think you're an unlikely suspect, ma'am. You were here for the funeral, right?"

Aunt E nodded. "They're burying my husband."

"My condolences." He turned to me. "So who are you? His son?"

"Almost, but no, Joe was my uncle. I flew down from New York."

"Okay, tell me more. What's your name and what do you do? And open your jacket."

I did so, glad that I'd left my gun back at West 35th Street. "My name's Archie Goodwin. I'm a private investigator."

He did a double-take. "Hold on! *The* Archie Goodwin? You work for that Wolfe guy?" He saw me nod. "Well, I'll be damned! I've read about you both. Wouldn't want Wolfe in my territory, but I wouldn't mind meeting him. Well, I've got work to do. You two stay right here."

He then walked over to the quartet of Tru-Sewn employees. It didn't take him long, though, before he made a general announcement that we all had to go to police headquarters.

I was glad that he told us we didn't need a police escort, but could drive there on our own. In the car with my aunt behind the wheel, I said that the absence of a police escort suggested that the inspector thought we must be in the clear.

"Well, of course! You only just arrived and as for me—"

"As for you," I cut in, "no matter how he feels, you can be sure he's going to check on whether you and Sam Marker had any of what my boss calls animus."

"That's ridiculous, Archie. Your uncle was quite fond of him and vice versa, as you heard. I asked him over a few times as our dinner guest and found him a dear man and utterly charming."

✗ ✗ ✗ ✗

At police HQ, we heel-cooled for a long time. Finally Inspector Yaeger clumped in looking the worse for wear and sat down across the table from us.

"Mrs. P," he said, "you're free to go home, but I'd like to talk to Archie for a while. I'll see that he gets a ride back afterward."

I agreed to stay. She waved goodbye and left.

When we were alone, Yaeger grumbled, "Not one of them has any motive for killing Marker."

"Are you sure about that?"

"Nope. I just couldn't uncover one. We'll have to start digging and God knows how long it'll take. Marker was not only popular, he was a community leader, and the Mayor owes his election largely to him. Which means I'm going to have him on my back if I can't solve this PDQ."

"Well, still, it's only four men."

"Yeah, but none of them have any survivors—would you believe?! This ain't gonna be easy. Still, they all knew Marker and they all were at the funeral."

"Did you find the gun?"

"We did. It was in the grass near where they were standing. We ran it over to Ballistics and it's the murder weapon, all right, but we couldn't lift any fingerprints."

"At least one of the other four must have seen something."

He shook his head and stuck another cigar in his mouth. "They were all looking up where the rifle squad was firing."

"Didn't anyone hear the fatal shot?"

"One is deaf and the others are all hard of hearing. What they did hear were twenty-one rifles being fired, that's it."

Coincidence sucks, I thought.

"Look, Goodwin, do you think you could get your boss to help?"

Grasping at straws. Or one fat straw.

"He wouldn't come here," I replied. "I could call him, but how much can you afford for his time and effort?"

"I'll buy him a case of beer."

I was going to discourage him when a possible hook occurred to me. I told him to bring me a phone.

His face lit up. He got a phone and stood by while I dialed.

"Yes?" Wolfe asked. I can never get him to answer properly. "Oh, it's you. You'll be home tomorrow, right?"

That was the hook I had in mind. "It all depends," I said.

"Depends on what?" Not quite a growl.

"I'm in a situation. Let me tell you about it."

Inspector Yaeger gestured for me to let him to talk to Wolfe, but I shook my head and laid a finger on my lips to keep him quiet.

"It's like this," I said and laid it out for him. I ended by saying that the Florida inspector asking his help had no budget to pay him, but would personally send him two cases of beer. (So I inflated it.)

"But," I added, "if you say no, I could be here a while longer."

A Wolfean equivalent of a laugh. "This will be the easiest fee I ever earned. It might make the beer taste better." He then told me what to pass along to the inspector.

It was the fastest case Nero Wolfe ever solved.

⚒   ⚒   ⚒   ⚒

Driving me to my plane, Aunt E asked, "Did your boss help that nice policeman?"

"He practically solved it for him. What he did was narrow it down to a single suspect, and once Inspector Yaeger knew who to focus on, it didn't take long to find out that the murderer believed Sam Marker caused his brother's death. Sam fired the brother from Tru-Sewn and that apparently drove the man to drink. He was drunk when he stepped in front of an oncoming truck."

"So what exactly did Mr. Wolfe say?"

"He told the inspector to find out whether any of the four were ever in the army and also whether any of them belonged to the American Legion."

"What would *that* mean?"

I told her to take the next highway turnoff. When we were on the right road, I explained that finding out about those things would suggest the killer's advance awareness that Uncle Joe's funeral would be military and thanks to the American Legion, there'd be a twenty-one gun salute that could cover up his own pistol shot.

✗   ✗   ✗   ✗

Wolfe was glad that I came back without any delay. He was even more pleased when the beer arrived. "Nordik Wolf!" he exulted. "Be sure to send my thanks to that inspector. Clearly, the man is no piker!"

✗

Marvin Kaye is the author of seventeen novels and numerous short stories, as well as the editor of best-selling anthologies, *Sherlock Holmes Mystery Magazine*, and *Weird Tales* magazine. A native of Philadelphia, he is a graduate of Penn State, with an M.A. in theatre and English literature.

GUTSY

by Laird Long

I'm a cheater, a weasel, a con-artist, a flim-flam man an' a loser. A big loser. But I ain't no murderer. What I got is a big yap. That's how come I got inta all this trouble. That's how come fear is drilling a hole in my gut you could drive a rig trew. If you could stomach the ride. I know I can't. I leak outta every orifice in my body.

It all started and ended when the cops caught me sellin' some paste to one of theirs. They slapped me around a lil' and I started cryin' like a baby and singin' like a canary on a low-seed diet. I just didn't wanta go back to the jug—I just got outta there tree weeks before, for God's sake. So I started yippin' about how I was in on all these murders, not as the trigger-man, of course, just as an interested observer, and how I could finger the boys who did 'em. Well, sweet Mary of mercy, afta I says that I got a parade of dicks from the FBI talkin' to me, promisin' me immunity, a new home, a new car, a new face, you name it. I ain't never been treated so good, you know, so I keeps up the charade.

Now I'm holed up in a cheap motel with two dicks waitin' to go to trial. Now I got fear eatin' away my stomach linin' like a bottle of Thunderbird.

I got the Mob afta me now. They think I might actually know somethin', or, at least, they can't take the chance that I do. I got a price on my coconut. I ain't never been worth so much to nobody in all my miserable life. An' to top it all off, they put the "Angel of Death" on the job. Angel Hammer, a.k.a. the "Angel of Death," a.k.a. "The Hammer," a.k.a. "The Unholy Ghost."

The Angel gets a million smackers a kill, for Christ's sake. He never misses. And I'm his next assignment—sorta like chum is the next meal for a shark. Ho' boy, I'm already dead unless I think of somethin' fast. The Angel always strikes at midnight, and it's 11:30 p.m. right now.

"We got men all over this dump, Skinny. Not to worry," the FBI dick named Cleaver says ta me.

"Honey, meet Cleaver." Ha, ha (meat cleaver, get it)! One thing I gots, it's a sense of humor, although right now I gotta tumor on that humor by the name of the Angel.

"He's right. We've got a small army guarding you. We've got as many men as guard the President of the United States," the other dick, Tubor, chimes in. I calls 'im "Potato." I got a million of 'em. And so does the Angel.

My mind drifts back to the shortened presidencies of Kennedy and McKinley and to the fine jobba protection provided to Reagan and Ford. For a wiseguy-wannabe, I know a bit about the world. I swaller down some of the eggs from supper that are comin' back up on me.

The dicks are watching *Apocalypse Now* on the boob tube and the nutcase Colonel says, "What do you call it when the assassins accuse the assassin?", and then they looks at me like I got an answer to that rhet-orical question. I runs to the can and pukes my guts out. That's my answer to just about anythin'. My body's as leaky as a tissue-paper condom.

11:45 p.m.

"You see anyone out there, Gordon?" Cleaver says to anudder dick out in the motel parkin' lot who's blowin' on a cup of joe to stay awake.

"Thought I heard something, but I checked it out and I couldn't find anything," the dick named Gordon crackles back ova the walkie-talkie.

Did it sound like wings? How do you stop the "Angel of Death?" That question's been batted aroun' long before I started wettin' my pants.

They're real mad at me out there to send the Angel. I gotta do somethin' or I ain't gettin' outta this alive. The only problem is, whenever I do somethin' on my own, I usually wind up gettin' screwed. That's why I like it when others do the thinkin' for me. I do think I'm gonna barf again.

I decides on a plan.

I step inta the bedroom of the two-bit suite and shut the door.

"Cleaver, come here, I need you!" I shout after a minute ticks by in slow-motion. Who the hell am I? Alexander friggin' Graham Bell?

It works, though. He opens the door and steps inta the room. I konks him on the noggin' wit the telephone receiver. He swoons on the bed, nice and quiet. Maybe things is gonna work out this time.

I steps outta the bedroom and Tubor looks up from the tube. He looks back at the tube and I konks him upside the head with the butt-end of Cleaver's gun—same M.O. I drags Cleaver outta the bedroom and prop him up in one of the chairs. I lay Howard down on the couch. I feel like tuckin' 'im in, he looks so peaceful. I saunter inta the ratty kitchen and pull a bottle of Heinz outta the cupboard. I smear the catsup all over their nice clean monogrammed white shirts—looks just like I shot 'em. Hope it does, anyway.

11:55 p.m.

I'm sweatin' lika bottle a beer at a Teamster's meetin'. My stomach is flippin' and floppin' lika Russian gymnast. I almost wish I was dead. Almost. One thing about Skinny, one thing I like more than anything else, and that's my worseless hide.

11:57 p.m.

The door to the motel room opens a crack and I sees a pair of wire choppers cut the chain on the door. I wanta scream. I soils myself, I'll admit it. I came inta this world wit a dirty diaper, now I'm goin' out wit one. Maybe.

The "Angel of Death" enters the room. He's early; just my luck.

He's a short pudgy guy with a pair of thick glasses and a thin mustache. He's dressed in a long black coat and he's gotta black fedora casin' his gourd. Someone should tell 'im to take it easy on the Bogie movies. He looks a little like Peter Lorre, only meaner.

He puts his hands in the pockets of his long black coat and stands in the middle of the cheap room lookin' at me and the two dicks sprawled out on the furniture like they're deceased. I'm so friggin' scared I can't even look up at 'im.

"Well, well, what do we have here?" he asks in a squeaky voice that fits his body. It's always the little guys who are the meanest—Napoleon, Himmler, Eddie Shore: the list is longer than the tapeworm I'm carryin' in my 'stines.

"I killed 'em both," I says in a quaverin' voice that I weren't fakin'. "I can't go trew wit it! I ain't no rat! Let me go and I'll clear out forever—you won't hear anudder word from me!"

"So they died for your sins, did they?" he says, wit just a hint of emotion. "Do you know why I'm here, Skinny?" he asks.

"Yeah, to blow me away!" I scream in a Shirley Temple voice. "But don't ya see, you don't have ta now!"

"No. I came here to protect you."

"What!?"

"Yes, indeed, Skinny. You see, you might think I'm just a faceless killer with the morals of a Sodom denizen—a spiritually bankrupt man in business only for the money."

"You pegged it, cousin," I squeals like Ned Beatty in *Deliverance*.

"But I live by a code. I live by His teachings."

Oh, great, I thought, a Jesus freak. That's the problem wit these hit-men, they got way too much time on their hands to think. They only work about ten hours every two weeks—they're worse than teachers, for God's sake.

He continued his sermon. "'The wrath of God is being revealed from heaven against all the godlessness and wickedness of men who suppress the truth by their wickedness.' I am the instrument of that wrath, Skinny. I am the truth."

The truth fairy. And I'm a bowl of orange jello. I decided to humor him since I wasn't goin' anywhere, 'cept maybe down.

"How come you work for the Mob, then?"

"I work for them and against them—if they want someone evil, someone of their own kind killed, I will do the job and be rewarded. I will do the job for them, for our own government agencies and even for foreign governments. As long as the individuals targeted are judged by me and through me, by the Lord, to be evil. I am controlled by no one but Him. I am also a bodyguard for the weak who are trying to stand up to the evil. Someone like yourself, Skinny. At least I thought you were someone like that, Skinny."

Friggin' great, I thinks to myself! I pull this dud sham to try to weasel outta gettin' killed by this guy, then he tells me he was sent by the Lord to protect me. Like I says, I'm a loser. Now he's probably goin' kill me 'cause he thinks I killed the dicks.

"Now the truth is revealed, Skinny. Now I find that you are the evil one, so shall you die."

"Wait! I just faked it, man! I couldn't murder anyone! I had crabs for two years 'cause I couldn't bring myself to kill 'em little guys!" I starts shakin' Cleaver, slappin' his kisser, tryin' to wake the stiff up.

"Stand away from the Dead!" the Angel shouts. "Have you no respect for the Dead, Wicked One?"

I gots more respect for the livin'. I throws the nut a screwgy.

"'If you are convinced that you are a guide for the blind, a light for those who are in the dark... you, then, who teach others, do you not teach yourself? You who brag about the law, do you dishonor God by breaking the law?'"

Like I said, I knows a bit about the world. I studied to become a priest for about six months 'cause I thought it would get me outta workin' for a livin'.

The Angel don't flinch. Instead his hands pop up from beneath his long coat right through the pockets and I sees they're holdin' two Glock 9 mms wit silencers. He's got all the answers. A bullet whistles outta one and slams inta my right shoulder, breakin' my collarbone. A.k.a. the surgeon, and his gun is his scalpel. He's gonna carve me up lika spam sanwich.

Just then, when he's targetin' my left shoulder and I'm cryin' lika dame stood up at the altar, Cleaver shakes the cobwebs outta his thick head and mumbles somethin'. The Angel moves over by his side to comfort him or to hear his confession.

Well, Cleaver sees the "Angel of Death" comin' towards him wit two rod in his mitts, comin' to get 'im he thinks, so he grabs his own rod an' plugs the Angel in the forehead. The Angel tumbles to the floor and breaks lika golden idol. That's gratitude for ya.

I takes advantage of this new development to make a run for the door.

"Hold up there, Skinny," Cleaver yells, "everything's under control."

I ain't even got my bladder under control yet. I keep hustlin' for the door and don't look back 'til I finally bust out of the dump.

✗   ✗   ✗   ✗

I been runnin' ever since. I think maybe, keep my pinkies crossed, that my luck may've changed. I got a nice job here in Columbia carryin' packages cross the border in my stomach. When I reach my contact, I got no trouble gettin' 'em out. Everyone's got a talent, right?

I probably shouldn'a blabbed so much to that nice guy who was buying me drinks last night, though. Someone told me he might be wit the DEA, whatever that stands fer.

✗

Laird Long: Big guy, sense of humor; pounds out fiction in all genres. Has appeared in many anthologies and mystery magazines and resides in Winnipeg, Canada.

THE BRIXTON JEWEL THEFT CAPER

by Jack Grochot

Informants and agents were sometimes deployed by my friend Sherlock Holmes whenever a mission precluded his direct involvement, principally because he might be recognised by a crime suspect despite numerous disguises or because the culprit might speak more candidly to a familiar face. Such was the case with the blithe Shinwell Johnson, a former convict known in the underworld as Porky and a valuable source of data to Holmes about nefarious doings. Then there was Mercer, "my general utility man," as Holmes described him. Add to them the youngster Wiggins, leader of a band of street Arabs that Holmes nicknamed the Baker Street Irregulars. Most memorable of the lot, however, was the lovely Miss Evelyn Pontier, a woman of the night from South London who brightened our Baker Street flat on occasion with tidbits, gossip and even solid evidence of wrongs committed by some of her many clients, ranging from the rich and powerful to the ordinary.

Miss Pontier, a gregarious brunette whose flowing silk dresses never failed to expose a well-turned ankle, and whose personality always suggested a coquettish quality, became a fixture in our apartment during Holmes's investigation of a counterfeiting ring in Brixton, her neighbourhood in the Borough of Lambeth.

"My famous, handsome confidant," she characteristically addressed him late one sunny autumn afternoon, "I have news for you that will cause you to shower me with affection. One of my admirers, a Mr Sidney Wayne of Haberdashery Row, called on me yesterday evening and left me with five one-pound notes that my banker this morning claimed were not genuine. The prude refused to accept them for deposit into my account. Oh, goodness, my dear, what is a poor working girl to do about such a calamity?"

Holmes cleared his throat and promised his confederate that he would pursue the incident with gusto, surmising the merchant more than likely received the notes from a customer at the shop where clothing and accessories were peddled. "Perhaps your caller would remember who paid him with those notes," Holmes suggested, expressing his gratitude for the lead in his inquiry. "In any event, I shall stress to the haberdasher that he owes you five pounds in bona fide currency."

"It is either that or I collect from his wife," Miss Pontier threatened in her distinct French accent. "I can be ruthless when it comes to satisfying a bad debt."

"I shall have Dr Watson remind me from time to time never to cross you, my sweet Evie," Holmes sputtered with mock respect. "It can be almost as dangerous as crossing me, you see."

"Perish the thought, my love," our visitor proclaimed, brushing her wavy light brown hair off her shoulder in a seductive manner and shaking her head no. With that, she rose from the settee with a flourish, blew us both a kiss and scampered toward the hallway. "Tata for now, boys, I am off to an exquisite dinner engagement," she sang.

After she departed, a hint of her expensive perfume still lingering, Holmes confided to me that he suspected Miss Pontier of entanglement in the counterfeiting scheme. "Her story of having been duped by Mr Sidney Wayne might be a ruse to throw me off the scent," he conjectured. "I believe her frequent appearances in our quarters could be attempts to gather intelligence on my progress—not to bring me worthwhile facts, but to charm me into revealing what I have discovered. A capital mistake in dealing with informants is to place trust in their implied motives. After all, these curious and often entertaining individuals are merely travelers among the criminal elements of our complex society."

"What makes you think the enigmatic Miss Pontier is a conspirator?" I asked while clearing the sitting-room of our tea pot and cups.

"Something she said and something she seems to have done," Holmes answered cryptically.

"Tell me more," I begged to hear.

"No counterfeiter would bother to reproduce a quid," Holmes went on. "A one-pound note is too small in denomination for the effort it takes to engrave a copy. The spurious notes in circulation are twenty pounders. Additionally, I witnessed during my surveillance of my prime suspect, Archie Stamford, the forger, a woman in a hooded jacket leaving his printing establishment. I followed her to the bawdy house in Brixton where Miss Pontier takes her clients, as do the other prostitutes I once interviewed in the case you recorded as 'the Deadly Goodge Street Affair.' I can't swear to it in court, but I would hazard a guess Miss Pontier was the hooded female in question."

"It appears your agent is playing both sides of the street," I commented.

"I shall know more after I speak with Mr Sidney Wayne tomorrow," Holmes speculated. "In the meantime, Watson, what say we walk to Simpson's, for the weather is enticing."

"A splendid idea!" I concurred, and donned my bowler.

Along the way, we stopped at the news stand in Cavendish Square for the evening edition of the *Daily Gazette*, the headline of which caught our attention. "Daring Robbery and Murder," it read, and beneath that, in smaller type: "Brixton Clerk Shot Dead as Jewels Are Stolen."

"Hmmm, fancy that, another mystery in Brixton," Holmes mused, rubbing his pointy chin and glancing at me with a frown on his gaunt face. "A peaceful location has morphed into a veritable hotbed of evil. You can read the details to me at our table."

I summarised each shocking paragraph as we sipped our glasses of port, a synopsis that included the puzzling circumstances of the clerk's killing and the statement that the shopkeeper, one Leander Gutkin, closed early for the day, locking the doors and windows. There was no sign of a forcible entry, I related, and nothing else was stolen except a diamond-studded tiara valued at eight hundred pounds and a ruby necklace worth about two hundred pounds. The clerk, Willard Tubbs, who left the store empty-handed with owner Gutkin, was found murdered at home nearly a mile from his place of employment, the news article disclosed. It mentioned also that the fatal bullet appeared to have been fired at a distance of less than a foot, a conclusion based upon evidence of a narrow pattern of powder-blackening on the victim's white shirt, according to Scotland Yard.

"The case slightly intrigues me, Watson, and I shall deem it suitable to step in only when Inspector Lestrade or one of his underlings comes to our door for assistance," Holmes remarked expectantly as I laid down the newspaper on the vacant chair beside me and savoured the steaming baked chicken breast with gravy that had been set before me alongside an ample mound of fluffy mashed potatoes and garden-fresh snap peas.

Our conversation during dinner and our walk home from the Strand was dominated by Holmes's recent obsession with the preposterous notion that the Benz Patent-Motorwagen would some day replace the horse-drawn carriage and revolutionise transportation around the world. "Imagine what havoc such a vehicle could produce in the hands of a criminal like Abner Sithebe, the notorious bank robber," said an anxious Holmes, cringing, as we reached our door on Baker Street.

Inside, Mrs Hudson, our landlady, accosted us at the foot of the stairs to apprise Holmes that Inspector Tobias Gregson was in our sitting-room, there to discuss an urgent matter that would not wait until morning.

"I took him up and we built a fire because I didn't want him to stand out in the chilly air until you returned, Mr Holmes," she explained. "I couldn't have invited him into my lodgings, since the ladies from my sewing circle are crowded into my parlour and, naturally, he would have been uncomfortable among a flock of chirping birds."

"You did the right thing, Mrs Hudson," I told her reassuringly. "Inspector Gregson is a welcome guest any time."

Regarded by Holmes as the smartest of the Scotland Yarders, the nattily-dressed and soft-spoken police official rose from an armchair near the hearth when we entered our diggings, a notebook in his one hand, a pencil in the other, with his wide-brimmed felt hat cocked back on his head. "Mr Holmes, Dr Watson, I hope you don't mind the intrusion," he began.

"Not at all, Inspector, I was expecting someone from the Yard before this, actually," said Holmes cheerfully as he hung his cape on the rack. "Trouble in Brixton brings you here, I suppose."

"More trouble than I care to withstand, Mr Holmes," Gregson retorted sternly. "The mayor himself has interfered in my investigation, demanding that we put a halt to the crime spree in such an upper-class and peaceful community. 'If the well-off in Brixton find themselves in jeopardy, think of how the common subjects in the remainder of the city must feel,' he complained to my superiors. Of course, if my supervisors undergo heat from above, they transfer the pressure to the detective on the street."

"Politicians and police work don't mix, in my estimation," Holmes groused. "The mayor needs to learn to stay clear of the detective business, unless he is prepared to handle the repercussions when the solution to the puzzle falls into his own territory."

"What are you suggesting, Mr Holmes?" Gregson queried with a surprised look.

"Only that I wouldn't be astonished if all the consternation in Brixton were somehow related and the villain was revealed to be a pillar of society," Holmes prophesied.

"Is that one of your inexplicable and brilliant deductions, then, Mr Holmes?" the admiring inspector intoned.

"I have a theory, but it is too premature to discuss, and all the data are not yet assembled," a coy Holmes answered. "Tell me what you have discovered in your probe thus far, Inspector, for I know only what has been published in the *Daily Gazette*."

"Well, the account in the newspaper is accurate, as it goes, but it is incomplete," Gregson averred. "I withheld a crucial piece of information from the reporters when they converged on the scene of the theft. It appears an intruder gained access to the jewelry shop by climbing down the chimney, like Saint Nick on Christmas Eve. I found traces of soot on the floor and footprints, which led to the glass case where the valuables were displayed. Our culprit is a dwarf, Mr Holmes, for only a tiny person would have been able to navigate the narrow opening."

"A palpable assumption," Holmes reasoned, "but have you considered the possibility it was a child?"

"A child, Mr Holmes?" a skeptical Gregson ejaculated. "Really, how could a child know the worth of a tiara and a necklace out of all the items from which to choose?"

"Easily, if he or she were instructed to steal only certain things," Holmes countered.

"It's a leap, for sure, but I dare not discount what you say, because you have been correct on many other more puzzling affairs," Gregson allowed. "I thought you might have a suspect in mind if you knew the offender was a dwarf, but your suggestion that it could have been a child has served to broaden the list."

"I do know of a burglar who is a miniature, Dennis Barber," Holmes acknowledged, "but I saw him only three days ago on crutches with his leg in a cast. He was hobbling out of Archie Stamford's printing shop."

"A crippled dwarf would not suffice as a suspect in this instance," Gregson stated, sounding disappointed. "Please give the situation more thought, Mr Holmes. Perhaps a second person will come to mind."

"Before you leave, Inspector, take a moment to describe the scene of the murder," Holmes proposed. "Was the clerk bound hand and foot, or was he free to move about, as I believe he might have been?"

"No, he was not tied. What does that tell us?" Gregson wondered.

"It tells us that Tubbs did not resist and knew his killer. Was the victim shot from behind?" Holmes questioned matter-of-factly.

"Why, yes, square in the centre of the back," Gregson marveled, running the palm of his hand across his forehead.

"It was someone who couldn't look him in the eye and dispose of him—probably a lover. Who discovered the body?" Holmes quizzed.

"Willard Tubbs's mother, who had gone to his house to do some cleaning," Gregson advised. "The dear lady was beside herself with fear and distress when I discussed the details with her."

"Was the house in disarray, or did she tidy up?" Holmes wanted to know.

"She had not yet lifted a finger when she came across the sight of her son prostrate in the parlour," Gregson continued.

"Then I expect his domicile had not been ransacked as if the killer were looking for something," Holmes further surmised.

"It was as neat as a pin," Gregson recalled.

"Excellent work, Inspector," Holmes complimented him. "There is no more to learn for now. Let us rendezvous at the jewelry store tomorrow at ten o'clock in the morning and by ten o'clock tomorrow night we might have the murderer in custody and the stolen property in hand."

"That should relieve the strain from above me," Gregson smiled.

He went on his way, whistling a merry tune down the stairs, when Holmes fished a half-smoked cigar from the coal scuttle, then settled into the wicker basket-chair, bemoaning the lack of truly challenging crimes to occupy his remarkable intellect.

"Does this mean you already know the identities of the killer and the jewel thief?" I pressed.

"I am positive of the outcome of Gregson's predicament, Watson, although I need more data to prove it in court," Holmes postulated. "Join me for a taste of brandy before we retire?" he offered, extending his arm toward the decanter on the tantalus.

✗   ✗   ✗   ✗

In the morning, we were aboard a train in route to Brixton as Holmes was transfixed on the rapidly passing scenery of gloomy and bright-coloured dwellings, factories with belching smokestacks, trees with fall foliage, pedestrians scurrying to their offices and conveyances delivering passengers to sundry addresses.

"How utterly inconspicuous and anonymous one can become among a population of millions," he observed with a casual glance toward me on the seat beside him. "Such was the situation when I conducted my surveillance on Archie Stamford's place of business, unnoticed on the park bench across the avenue. There was no indication then that the counterfeiting caper would merge with the investigation of a jewel depredation and murder several days later." Ever the type who played his cards close to his vest, Holmes spoke no more of the coincidental connection.

We intentionally arrived early for our appointment with Gregson so that Holmes would have the time to interview haberdasher Sidney Wayne and the banker who rejected the counterfeit notes presented by Miss Pontier. The clothing and accessories shop being only a short distance from the bank, we walked between the two establishments in a matter of minutes.

At Mr Wayne's, Holmes learned from the astounded and embarrassed proprietor that the one-pound notes he tendered to Miss Pontier had been withdrawn by him from the very bank, Thomas and Company, where the convivial and chatty informant secured her profits.

"So the money could not have been fake currency because it came out of a teller's drawer, Mr Holmes," Wayne confided sheepishly. "Lord help me if my wife finds out about my liaison with another female. Please, please, Mr Holmes, be discreet and circumspect with the confession I have made to you."

"Your secret is safe with me, be confident of that, Mr Wayne," Holmes whispered to soothe the distraught gentleman's anxiety.

The head teller at Thomas and Company remembered clearly the transaction with Miss Pontier, telling Holmes she attempted to deposit five suspicious notes in denominations of twenty pounds each. "The engraving on them was flawless, but the paper itself was too thin and rough," he said, winking. "She is an attractive young lady, but not a good pretender. She made a fuss about my decision and maintained she would withdraw all her funds if I didn't accept the deposit. She left the bank in a huff after speaking to the manager, who, in the end, agreed with me and told her he would notify the police."

"I can be certain now," Holmes boasted on our way out of the bank, "that she was the hooded figure I followed from Archie Stamford's and she fabricated a tale about one-pound notes."

It approached the ten o'clock hour as Holmes and I traversed the two blocks to meet Inspector Gregson at jeweler Leander Gutkin's establishment, a broad luxurious shop with an interior that featured a plush hand-woven carpet imported from India and walls decorated by original oil paintings from the hands of contemporary French and German masters.

Gutkin was none too pleased with all the attention from the police. He also objected to the presence of Holmes and an insurance investigator from Lloyd's of London, which carried a loss policy on the stolen merchandise. "This interference in my routine is a detriment to my business," Gutkin grumbled to Gregson. "Can't all this wait until after hours?" Gutkin moaned.

"Have mercy, Mr Gutkin, your loyal employee was murdered just yesterday, probably because he could identify the thief," Gregson reproved. "We have a valid reason for what we are doing at this time of day."

Holmes, meanwhile, was engaged in a quiet conversation with the Lloyd's representative, Winship Seward, and took him out onto the walkway to exchange words in private. When they came back inside, Holmes examined the case where the pilfered jewels were usually locked and inquired of Gutkin how the intruder could have made off with the tiara and necklace without breaking the glass.

"I had them out on the counter to show a customer and apparently forgot to turn the key once she left the store," Gutkin guessed. "All the other valuables were locked up and that must be why nothing else was stolen."

"Yet I am perplexed—the tiara and necklace were the only valuables insured by Lloyd's, is that not correct?" Holmes queried.

"Yes, because the remainder of my uninsured inventory is worth far less and Lloyd's was the only consortium willing to take the risk on those two pieces," Gutkin explained.

Holmes then began a close inspection of the fireplace and the small footprints in soot on the floor, halting twice to sniff the air in opposite areas of the store. "Midnight Encounter, from Paris," he said to me under his breath. "A familiar fragrance, is it not?"

My nostrils detected nothing, due to years of pipe smoking and exhaling through my proboscis.

Finished at the jeweler's, we rode in a growler to the residence of the deceased clerk. We entered his second-floor apartment with a key that Gregson obtained from Willard Tubbs's mother the day before. Holmes sniffed the air again, his hawk-like countenance tilted upward as we came together in the middle of the parlour where the corpse had lain.

"It is the identical scent," he observed, running his bony fingers through his straight dark hair. "If I deduce accurately, the assailant fired the fatal bullet from a single-barrel derringer," Holmes prognosticated to an awe-struck Gregson.

The inspector muttered to himself and suggested we attend the autopsy that morning to validate Holmes's conclusion by determining the calibre of the bullet.

"A prescient suggestion," said Holmes immediately, "because that was my next thought."

"We have gone through the victim's belongings with a fine tooth comb and could find no clue," Gregson recited. "Perhaps your eyes will produce a different result."

Holmes dropped to his hands and knees with his convex lens and scoured the floor, then the furniture, moving from room to room and finally to the bed, where, on a pillow, he located a long strand of hair the hue of polished oak.

"A woman in his life, no doubt," Holmes murmured, carefully placing the specimen in an envelope that he carried in his jacket pocket. "A derringer, or stocking pistol, is a woman's preferred weapon for self-defence. Let us travel to Saint Bart's for the post mortem."

As we rode the Underground to the great hospital, Holmes enthralled Gregson and me with stories about violent *femme fatales* throughout history in foreign countries, where hanging or beheading or stoning the vicious offenders was not uncommon.

The autopsy of Willard Tubbs was in progress when we reached the dissecting room of Saint Bart's and Dr Uttley already had removed a .41-calibre bullet that pierced the young man's aorta and lodged in his sternum.

"The projectile is intact and bears a distinct imperfection," Gregson stated upon examining it, "so if we seize a firearm from a suspect, we can definitely use your latest method to make an accurate comparison to a test bullet. You were precisely on the mark, Mr Holmes, a palm gun did him in. What is our next move—to search for a woman?"

"Leave that to me," Holmes instructed. "You can concentrate on the jewel theft, for that link to the killing will establish the motive, which, at the moment, we lack."

Gregson went on his way back to Brixton as Holmes tore a blank sheet of paper from his notebook to compose a message that he asked me to deliver to Peterson, the commissionaire, on my trip to Baker Street.

"I shall meet you at our flat in roughly two hours, Watson, because I must first round up Shinwell Johnson for an important chore I cannot perform myself," he explained.

I took a cab to Peterson's office and told the commissionaire to deliver the message promptly because time was of the essence. Next, I went across the busy thoroughfare to a café to enjoy a basket of fish and chips, for I was famished. Later, there was a lively concert by four street musicians playing guitars and mandolins down the block, so I sat on a low stone wall and listened to their melodies for a long while. Afterward, I stopped at the Great Peter Street post office to send a letter I had been toting in my jacket for days, then strolled leisurely home to wait for Holmes. But he had arrived before me and was entertaining a Miss Penelope Cartier, another occupant of the bawdy house in Brixton, where she plied her trade in a room adjacent to Miss Pontier's.

Miss Cartier was leaving as I reached the top of the steps and Holmes introduced us as he accompanied her down to hail a cab. Holmes returned to our quarters in a chipper mood, jabbering about his visitor and her infinite capacity for trivia. He said she rushed to see him after receiving his message all awash with minutiae about Leander Gutkin and Miss Pontier.

"He is a frequent guest at the house of ill repute, and Miss Cartier was not reticent about his arrogant behaviour there," Holmes related. "She furnished information a-plenty to cook his goose whenever I lower the net on him," he prophesied with a grin.

Holmes changed the subject and peppered me with questions about Cornwall, a prelude to our adventure there in the upcoming days to solve the mystery of the missing lighthouse keepers. Our dialogue was interrupted by a ring of the doorbell and a frenzied Mrs Hudson clamouring at our threshold to announce the arrival of a portly bloke who told her he had urgent business with Holmes.

"He says his name is Porky Johnson and the matter is confidential," she sniffed.

"I have been eager to hear from him, Mrs Hudson, so send him up," Holmes ordered.

Huffing and puffing from the climb, Shinwell Johnson scratched his bald scalp under his navy blue knit cap and hesitated. "I didn't know you'd be with somebody, Mr Holmes, so I'll wait down under the lamppost until your company leaves," he squawked.

"Nonsense, Porky, you can say now whatever is on your mind, because Dr Watson is a trusted colleague who will honour your confidential role in this escapade."

"Whatever you want, Mr Holmes, as long as my name stays out of this and my information earns me the crown you promised," the nervous agent said cautiously.

"Archie Stamford is your man, for sure, because he shows me a stack of twenty-pound notes and offers to sell them to me for ten pounds apiece. Then he goes into a back room and comes out with a tiara and a necklace. He asks me if I know of a contact in the underworld who would pay five hundred pounds for both. So I asks him where he gets such costly gems and he claims he buys them at a bargain from a lady friend."

"Wonderful, Porky, you have earned a bonus," Holmes praised. "Here is your crown and a sovereign for good measure."

"Blimey, Mr Holmes, you are the generous one," Johnson blurted and lumbered out the door.

Holmes wrung his sinewy hands in what I thought was anticipation of a confrontation with Stamford, but instead he focused his attention on the gregarious Evelyn Pontier and shopkeeper Gutkin.

"I believe Miss Evie and he were in league to defraud Lloyd's of London by staging the theft of the jewels and collecting a substantial settlement from the insurer," Holmes deduced, handing me my derby and putting on his top hat. "Shall we see if my conjecture can be authenticated?"

✗ ✗ ✗ ✗

We traveled again to Lambeth, where Holmes led me to the printing establishment operated by Stamford, a wiry unpleasant individual with a black goatee, mutton chops, and thick spectacles. He wore an apron stained with ink blotches that also dotted his shirt sleeves.

"Sherlock Holmes! The meddling viper that sent me to prison!" Stamford shouted as we came through the door. "You are not welcome here!"

"That was the first time you went to prison, Archie, but I'm afraid not the last," Holmes shot back. "Unless, of course, you cooperate with me and I put in a good word for you with the judge."

"You have me convicted already, Holmes, but for what crime I don't know," Stamford reacted. "Is this gent tagging along with you another copper?"

"No, this is Dr Watson, my biographer and associate, who is about to publicise your counterfeiting scheme," Holmes contended. "He knows all about it because the notes you produce bear your fingerprints."

"That is impossible, because I wear gl—" Stamford started to protest.

"Gloves, Archie?" Holmes prodded. "You are a talented forger, but not the most clever."

"What do you mean when you say I could cooperate and stay out of the penitentiary?" Stamford cajoled Holmes to elabourate.

"Now you are talking with your brains," Holmes commended. "Tell me about the transactions you made with Evie Pontier, but don't quit with the five notes you sold to her at first. Don't fail to mention the jewels."

"Come, now, Holmes, who is the rat? How could you know about the jewels unless there was a rat with a big mouth," Stamford pleaded.

"There was no rat, Archie, because I have been watching you from the other side of the street for many days," Holmes bluffed.

"Well, then, I need not tell you, if you have seen us with your two hawk eyes," Stamford barked.

"I need to hear it from your own lips and then listen to you testify in court before I recommend clemency on your behalf, Archie," Holmes said to encourage the truth.

"You're a bloomin' blackmailer, Holmes," Stamford quarreled, uttering a curse.

"A bloomin' extortionist, Archie. That is the more precise terminology," Holmes debated.

"Whichever you are, I suppose I have no choice," Stamford snarled. "She came in here with the goods and insisted she inherited them from her dearly departed aunt. But when I challenged her and mentioned these items were identical to the ones in the newspaper, she admitted they were as hot as a firecracker and implored me never to tell where they came from. I gave her a hundred of my fresh notes and pledged to keep quiet when I unloaded the jewels on a buyer in the underworld."

"Fetch the contraband, Archie, and I shall explain to Scotland Yard that it came from a confidential source whose name I cannot reveal," Holmes assured. "As for printing the phony notes, my word is my bond when you go before a judge."

Holmes and I left the shop with the tiara and necklace to locate Inspector Gregson in Brixton, finding him at the local constabulary questioning a six-year-old precocious boy known in the neighborhood as a shoplifter and member of a street gang, The Gnomes.

"And how much did they pay you, Jeremy?" the inspector was overheard interrogating the lad.

"The woman paid me four shillings, and the man gave me this special coin from Spain," Jeremy recollected, displaying a common peso excitedly. "It was easy work, just climb the elm tree, jump onto the roof, and shinny down the chimney, then out the door, shebang, g'bye."

"And can you swear you would recognise them again?" Gregson added.

"I'll never forget them as long as I live. Four shillings and a precious coin! How lucky I am," the happy little youngster crowed.

"I see you captured your burglar," Holmes remarked to Gregson, whose grey eyes sparkled when he set his gaze upon the diamond-studded tiara and ruby necklace. "Dare I inquire as to where these were confiscated, Mr Holmes?" he croaked.

"For the time being, be satisfied to learn they have been recovered from a cooperative fence who will testify against the party offering the gems to him," Holmes answered coyly.

"Who would that party be, then?" Gregson pursued further.

"A double-crossing hussy, Miss Evelyn Pontier, who often entertains Leander Gutkin in her room on Pinchin Lane," Holmes stated nonchalantly. "I have a plan to arrest both of them together for swindling the insurance syndicate and her in particular for the slaying of Willard Tubbs."

Gregson huddled with Holmes to discuss his stratagem and they parted company. Holmes then gave me an assignment—to venture over to Pinchin Lane, down near the water's edge, to convey a warning from public health officials to the operator of the bawdy house, Madame Adrienne Anastasie. She answered my knock at the carved oak door and invited me to have a seat on the sofa.

"This is not a social call—I am here on important business, Madame Anastasie," I informed her. "I am a physician, Dr John H Watson, empowered by the government to shutter your establishment to prevent any male callers from entering."

"This is drastic!" she spouted. "Why would you do this?"

"Because I have examined one of your clients and diagnosed him to be suffering from the Great Scourge, syphilis. I suspect he was infected by one of the ladies you employ," I continued with the bold fabrication.

"One of my girls? Which one, then?" Madame Anastasie demanded.

"It is difficult to accuse one right now. The man has been with several, he tells me," I went on.

"Who is this man? What is his name?" she pleaded.

"His name is Leander Gutkin, a jeweler from Brixton," I lied.

"Him! I should have known," she sneered. "What can I do about it? What will you do?"

"You can send to Dr Verner the women with whom Mr Gutkin has been in contact so they can be examined to single out the one who carries the disease," I advised. "In the meantime, I shall have a constable stationed at your door to discourage any more trade."

"Oh, me, this is a terrible thing you say you must do," she whimpered. "I will first send Evie, she is his favourite, then Angeline and Diana—they are the only ones."

"Here is Dr Verner's address in Kensington, Madame Anastasie," I said sympathetically, tearing a sheet out of my notebook. "Sorry to bring you such distressing information. Good day to you," I concluded.

"Not good, not good at all," she griped, sulking.

Meanwhile, Holmes was on his way to the office of Dr Verner, a distant relative of Holmes and the physician who had purchased the medical practice from me. Holmes would impose a request upon Dr Verner to vacate his office. Any patients who might visit there would be directed to find their doctor in his auxiliary rooms at Saint Bart's.

Inspector Gregson at the same time sought out Gutkin to upset him with a story similar to mine, advising him that one of his consorts had contracted syphilis and that Dr Verner was expecting him to report for an examination before the office closed at six in the evening. Gregson then joined Holmes, who occupied the waiting area at Dr Verner's. Gregson stepped into the examining room and hid from view.

Miss Pontier arrived before Gutkin, flabbergasted to see Holmes. "What are you doing here, my handsome confidant?" she wanted to know.

"I arranged for us to meet like this, my sweet Evie, because I wish to confront you alone with the results of my investigation," Holmes apprised her.

"But where is Dr Verner? I came to see him, not you, my darling," she replied, confused.

"Dr Verner is away. I am the only person here, my apologies," said he to deceive her.

"Is this a trick, then?" she wondered.

"Not as much of a trick as you played on me, on Lloyd's of London, and on the lifeless Willard Tubbs," Holmes alleged. "I cautioned you not to cross me because it could be dangerous."

"I insist on an explanation, Holmes," she mumbled nervously, near panic.

"Then I'll give you one, more than one, actually," he asserted. "To start, you obtained counterfeit money from Archie Stamford. Then you conspired with Leander Gutkin to simulate a burglary at his jewelry store. A street urchin named Jeremy will identify you two in court as the persons who gave him coins to climb down the chimney. You took the missing tiara and necklace to Stamford and obtained more bogus notes. And, finally, you murdered Mr Tubbs with the derringer you carry in your garter on the inside of your left thigh—your housemate Miss Cartier has seen it there and on your dresser when you sleep."

"You mean this derringer?" she snickered, snatching the weapon from her leg and pointing it at Holmes.

"Now be careful with that!" Holmes bellowed. "I'll not turn my back to you like Mr Tubbs did after discovering you and Gutkin were partners in crime."

"You can't prove it at all, my famous detective—it is supposition," she charged.

"I have evidence to support it," Holmes snorted. "I sensed your unmistakable perfume, Midnight Encounter, in the jeweler's shop and in Willard Tubbs's apartment. Your hair on his pillow matches one that you left on the settee at Baker Street. I have confirmed it microscopically. And a test bullet from your gun will compare nicely to the one removed from Mr Tubbs's cadaver."

"And the one they will extract from yours," Miss Pontier snapped.

"Not if I shoot you first!" Gregson shouted at the top of his lungs, thrusting himself into the fray with his revolver aimed at her pretty head. "Now hand over that pistol or I'll pull the trigger."

The frightened and stunned lawbreaker began to sob. "Don't hurt me," she whined. Then she lowered the derringer to her side, whereupon Holmes reached out and pried it loose from her grip.

"God forgive me for what I have done," she cried. "I didn't go to Willard's with the intention of killing him. I was intimate with him and tried to coax him into sharing in our little game. He refused and threatened to tell the police. He said he was an honest man. Something came over me suddenly and I was driven to silence him. He turned away from me and told me to get out."

At that moment, Leander Gutkin opened the door, witnessing Miss Pontier weeping, Gregson holding a revolver and Holmes the derringer. Gutkin spontaneously emitted a groan and stammered: "I-I-I was an innocent pawn in a plot conceived by that-that manipulator, that she-devil."

"Jurors will laugh at such a defence," Gregson howled. "A sad pair of connivers is what you are."

Holmes wiped the perspiration from his forehead with his handkerchief and together with Gregson marched the reprobates out of Dr Verner's office, then into a standing carriage that a constable positioned around the corner.

"When you told me your plan, Mr Holmes, it didn't include nearly getting shot," Gregson jested after his prisoners were secured in the vehicle.

"My plan did include a precaution, inspector," Holmes clarified. "I persuaded her friend, Miss Cartier, to empty the chamber of the derringer while Miss Pontier was snoozing during her usual afternoon nap."

✗

Jack Grochot is a retired investigative newspaper journalist and a former federal law enforcement agent specializing in mail fraud cases. He has written three books of Sherlock Holmes pastiches and a fourth nonfiction book, *Saga of a Latter-Day Saddle Tramp*, a memoir of his five-year horseback journey across twelve states. Grochot lives on a small southwestern Pennsylvania farm, where he writes and oversees a horse-boarding stable. This story is included in the book *Curious, eh, Watson?* He can be contacted by e-mail: grochot@comcast.net.

ABOVE SUSPICION

by Victoria Weisfeld

Boston, Conley Terminal, Sunday, March 18, 1990

Shortly before 9 a.m., Amit Madoor and his nephew Rashid arrived at the Port of Boston's Conley Terminal in two vintage Cadillacs. Dockhands directed them to park in a cavernous prep bay, where they emptied the cars' gasoline tanks and disconnected their batteries. A tow-truck maneuvered the two beauties into the open mouth of a steel shipping container and the workers clambered in behind to pack protective padding around and between them. End-to-end, the Caddies just about filled the forty-foot box.

Before the container was sealed, every dockworker having a spare minute strolled over to admire these cars—classics from 1956 and 1959—one purple and the other two-tone, turquoise and white. They peered through the windows at the immaculate leather upholstery, ran their hands over the fins and admired the wide whitewall tires. If circumstances allowed, they would have popped the hoods to check out the 325-horsepower engines. Drifting back to their work, they slapped each other on the back, recalling the hand-me-down cars of their youth. Every man of them would fantasize about these gleaming chariots, but they embodied no man's dreams more than Amit Madoor's.

✗   ✗   ✗   ✗

As soon as the container door clanged shut, Rashid said, "Gotta go. Noon clinic."

They embraced, the younger man kissing his uncle on both cheeks.

Madoor reached inside his suit jacket and pulled out his wallet. "Here. Please. Take some dollars for a taxicab."

"No. Thanks." Rashid pushed the bills away. "I'll jog partway, then catch the T to the hospital."

"Take a cab." Madoor nudged the money toward him, but Rashid ignored it.

"Uncle Amit, it was great to see you." Rashid reached out to shake his uncle's hand. Rashid was still in medical training, while Madoor, despite the closeness in their ages, wore his business-man's responsibilities like an extra overcoat.

"Thank you for your help," he said. "I will be always in your debt."

"Travel safely and maybe I'll visit you in Rome when my residency is finally over."

"I hope that you will. Be well."

Rashid jogged away, returning to his world of lecture halls and laboratories, the dwindling ill and the kinetic young doctors. When he was out of sight, Madoor turned back to the dock. His container, inspected and sealed, awaited pickup. The word "Evergreen" stenciled on its side seemed auspicious to him, a Muslim man.

He stood just inside the doorway of a low building and watched until the tall post-Panamax crane winched his container into the air, swung it into position and settled it on one of the rising stacks of red, yellow, green and blue containers like rust-streaked Lego bricks. None of the longshoremen were near enough to see his gloved hands clenching and unclenching or hear his long exhale once the container was safely aboard ship. Now it rested, hidden in plain sight among hundreds of others already loaded onto the *Annamarie*, scheduled for departure at noon Tuesday for the free port of Trieste.

He turned from the dock and walked toward the exit. Sirens in the distance slowed his steps, but when their shrill screams faded, he hurried on his way.

✗   ✗   ✗   ✗

Boston, Sunday, February 18, 1990

A month before their early morning on the docks, Madoor and his nephew walked along the snowy strip of parkland bordering the Charles River Basin. A few puffing joggers and a well-bundled dog walker were the only other people braving the snow-streaked path. Even so, they kept their voices low and said little more than necessary.

"You asked me to find two physician residents who are—what word did you use? Daring?" Rashid said. "I have them! Real cowboys. Technically, they're good surgeons, but they have that extra dose of confidence, that 'I can do anything' arrogance surgical specialists are prone to."

"If a doctor is planning to cut into me, I do not want him to have doubts!"

"As long as he's right."

"Yes. As you say, technically skilled."

"I don't know—don't need to know—why you want them, but these two are special. They do high-risk procedures all day, every day. As our residency director says, 'nerves of steel.'"

"A valuable trait. But would they be willing to help a stranger? All I can offer them is money." Madoor studied the ice clogging the river, willing one particular piece to break free. Rid of this one obstacle, the rest of the ice would flow freely to Boston Harbor, just as finding the right doctors would put his plans in motion.

"That's the other thing. They're totally obsessed about the state of their finances. That's not unusual. Most doctors leaving training worry about their debt. But these two never stop talking about it."

"How well do they know you? I don't want them to suspect our connection."

"They're a couple years ahead of me, so I'm invisible to them. Plus, I'm in general medicine, not surgery."

"Do they get along? Or are they competitors?" He watched the chunk of ice jostle its neighbors, slip past them and begin to move swiftly in the current.

"Actually, they're in different specialties. One's a neurosurgeon—"

"Neuro—?"

"Brain," Rashid said, "—and the other, orthopedics. Bones. And they're friends."

Madoor removed a glove to reach into his trouser pocket and pull out something small. He took Rashid's hand and closed it around the object.

"What's this?" Rashid asked, opening his gloved palm. On the black leather shone a platinum ring set with a carved crystal.

"For you. Your grandfather wants you to have it."

"Wow." Rashid held the ring up sideways, allowing sunlight to pass through the dome of the crystal. "It's beautiful."

"He is very proud of you. As am I. You will do great things, Rashid."

"Thank you, Uncle. He's been generous to us both. Paying my medical tuition. Helping you buy your shop."

"If we were not already determined to be successful, we would want to make something of ourselves just for him." Madoor paused. "He is dying, you know."

"The cancer is back?"

"Yes, your grandmother says he will be gone before summer. Which is why he is doing these last things for us, these last gifts." He gestured to the ring in Rashid's hand.

"We should bring him here." Rashid swung around to gaze at the looming Massachusetts General Hospital complex, as if a miracle lay waiting behind those stone and glass façades.

"You know he will not leave Fez. He is at peace there, surrounded by people who love him."

Rashid swallowed hard a time or two. "He has helped so many."

"Yes, he has." Madoor didn't mention the extra generosity his father recently extended to him—partly in the form of a loan and partly in something even more valuable, contacts—or the heavy obligation he felt to use them well.

⚹　⚹　⚹　⚹

Wednesday, February 28, 1990, noon

"What would you do if you had a million dollars?" Madoor asked the two surgical residents. They agreed to a quick lunch of sandwiches and coffee in a bustling Fruit Street diner hard by Massachusetts General Hospital on the strength of a "business proposition" Madoor said he hoped to tell them about.

He came to their meeting wearing a three-piece charcoal wool suit with a precisely knotted silver-gray tie and shoes shined that morning, whereas they wore wrinkled green cotton scrubs too thin for the weather and open-backed clogs. He'd folded his overcoat over an empty chair and his hat occupied the seat. The knitted sleeve-ends of the doctors' slippery down jackets thrown onto the backs of their chairs now trailed in dirty puddles of slush.

They looked run ragged, especially Jack, the neurosurgeon-in-training. Isaac, the orthopedics resident, was taller, younger and less intense. By lunchtime, they said, they'd been on their feet six hours already and they described some of the intricate repairs made to the brains and bones of their patients. They put in this level of effort, even though emergency cases kept them at the hospital until nearly one a.m. the night before.

"A million dollars!" The residents said together and burst out laughing. People at neighboring tables glanced over, including Madoor's nephew Rashid. The two surgeons, confident they knew everything important that was relevant to their lives, did not know about Madoor's relationship to one of their fellow trainees, nor that Rashid hand-picked them from the hospital's white-coated flock and told his uncle how to contact them.

"I am serious," Madoor said. His smile was sufficient to show good humor, crinkling the skin around his black eyes, but not enough to suggest he might be joking.

They regarded him closely, jutting out their chins and narrowing their gaze, as if trying to establish a diagnosis, though Madoor already observed much more about them than they would ever learn about him. Jack leaned far back in his chair and drummed the table a few times with the flat of his hands. Quietly now, he said, "Christ, Isaac, I think maybe he is."

"In my dreams," Isaac said and took another bite of a tuna on rye.

Jack leaned across his half-eaten sandwich. "I can tell you what I'd do with a million. I'd pay off my medical school loans and be a free man—free to start my own practice, free to move to San Diego. I'd dump that piece-of-shit hatchback, get a decent car and tool around Southern California with the top down. Man, I'd be set. Instead of a long slog trying to stay ahead of the debt-collector." He turned to his friend. "You?"

"I'd buy a really great apartment back home in Florida. Miami Beach. I'm thirty years old, for Chrissake. My fiancée and I want to get married, but she's not moving up here, that's for damn sure." He glanced out the window at the snow, coming down harder now, obscuring the dirty slush and treacherous patches of sidewalk ice.

"Thirty? I'm almost thirty-five and I don't even have a girl-friend," Jack said.

"What happened to—"

"She broke up with me. Said I never had time for her. Which is true." He pulled a disgusted face. "And my career's not even started. I won't dig out from under for years, while you're down in Miami rebuilding the hips and shoulders of all those old farts."

"The possibility interests you then?" Madoor said.

"The possibility interests me like winning the lottery interests me," Jack said, keeping his voice low. "But it ain't happening. Isaac's family, they could stake him, but not mine."

"But they won't." Isaac turned to Madoor. "My family thinks I'll make millions as an orthopedic surgeon and maybe someday I will. But I need money to get started." He pushed his empty plate away.

"You could have it." Madoor smiled. "I will gladly tell you how. But only if you have the nerve to go after it. Not everyone would. Please think how much easier your lives could be."

"For doing what, exactly?" Isaac asked.

Madoor shook his head. "When I tell you, it won't sound as dramatic or as worrisome as whatever you are thinking right now. It will be—easy. But first I must be sure that you are willing."

The waitress brought the check and Madoor reached for it. He opened his wallet and gave each of them a card from the Copley Plaza, his room number written on the back.

"Thank you for your time. I know my request to meet you was uncomfortably vague. And still is. But it will not be for long, depending on you."

"Hey, we had to eat," Jack said. He stirred his coffee.

"Good afternoon, gentlemen. I hope we meet again." Madoor walked to the cash register, pulling on his coat and positioning the trilby over his black hair. He shoved a tip in the jar and walked out into the snowstorm.

✗   ✗   ✗   ✗

Boston, Early March, 1990

In the following days, while Madoor waited to see whether the residents would take the bait, he walked the city, including its run-down industrial areas. He explored streets with small workshops, listening for noisy hammering and the whine of band saws, following the smell of motor oil and hot metal that flowed out when the rolling doors rattled up. He was in search of a special kind of neighborhood, one like those of his Moroccan childhood, and someone with particular skills.

Evenings he stayed in his hotel room, ordered room-service dinners and chuckled over his reading of Salman Rushdie's *The*

Satanic Verses. He was more than a hundred pages in when the phone rang. The surgeons wanted to talk again. Madoor suggested they meet in the Public Garden near the "Make Way for Ducklings" sculpture, the line of eight bronze ducklings trailing their mother at the edge of the park lawn.

At the appointed time the next day, a Saturday, they found a bench to share and Madoor described what they would have to do. He studied their reactions as they grasped the implications of his plan and for a few moments he thought it possible he would lose them. But his logic was persuasive. The job was simple. It entailed no violence. Everything was worked out. They just needed to follow the steps.

It would require two hours of their time at most, after which they could resume their normal lives, lives that would be so much easier with a million dollars apiece in special bank accounts, about which questions would never be raised. He stopped talking and let them think. From their body language, he was soon convinced they were talking themselves into it. Jack first.

"You know," Jack said, "most people don't have any idea about the huge amount of debt we end up with—from medical school and then from the low salaries we get as residents. Boston is expensive. And we're not living like kings, I assure you."

His friend snorted and Madoor nodded thoughtfully.

"Then we have to decide whether to go into practice by ourselves—and that costs a bundle—real estate, hiring people, equipment, getting set up, malpractice insurance, marketing—or join some existing practice. In my specialty—Isaac's, too—we're probably better off going in with someone. But it's a gamble how that relationship will work out."

Madoor watched a couple of determined pigeons trail a child eating a cookie.

"We'll be the low men on the totem-pole for a few *more* years. Medicaid patients, on-call," Jack said.

Madoor had no idea what he was talking about, but nodded again.

"But if we went into an existing practice with something in our hand—you know, technology they don't typically have—*plus* the experience using it, then we could negotiate."

"Get a *much* better deal," Isaac said.

"We have the most spectacular technology right here. If we could offer to replicate a piece of it, we'd be really value-add."

They thought a few minutes longer. Finally Jack stretched his arms across the back of the bench and squinted up into the wan spring sunshine filtering through the trees' still-bare branches. "We can do this."

"Well, sure we *can*." Isaac's emphasis was an unspoken "But should we?"

"Isaac, c'mon, man. It's a fucking gift from God." Jack slapped the bench. "I've put my life on hold long enough. San Diego, dude!"

Isaac leaned over, staring at his dirty boots.

A mother and her bundled-up twins wove in and out among the ducklings, laughing. The children ran past the bench where the men sat, splashing muddy slush onto Isaac, even getting some in his hair.

He brushed off the wet stuff and turned to Jack, grinning. "A great *big* gift from God." He was in.

A quote from Rushdie came to Madoor. It was about how men use God to justify the unjustifiable. And how so often, as in the present case, God has nothing whatever to do with it. He kept this thought to himself.

Now that the surgeons agreed to perform the job, Madoor set his hook with various assurances and payment details. They didn't waver. In their minds, he thought, the money was already spent.

✗　✗　✗　✗

Sunday, March 18, 11 a.m.

On the morning that Madoor watched the steel containers being loaded onto the *Annamarie*'s deck, dazed officials of the Isabella Stewart Gardner Museum wandered its Italianate galleries clutching clipboards and mumbling to Boston police detectives. FBI investigators were on their way and the media frenzy over the largest property theft in history was about to explode.

"So what's missing?" Detective Morris Kahn asked the curator stumbling along beside him. "We've been all over this place."

She checked the list recorded in her shaky handwriting and ticked off the losses. Five paintings: one of only about thirty-five known Vermeers, two Rembrandts, a Manet, a Flinck. Works on paper: a Rembrandt self-portrait the size of a postage stamp and five Degas drawings, three featuring horses. A three-thousand-year-old Chinese bronze beaker and, oddest of all, an eagle-shaped finial snatched from atop a Napoleonic banner.

She swallowed hard. "It looks like they couldn't pry the banner frame itself off the wall.... Too many screws." Her voice disappeared into a whisper.

"What's the value of all this?"

She brushed at her eyes. "Priceless."

Kahn and his detectives pieced together the story of the theft from the physical evidence, the hard drive of the motion detector equipment and their interviews with the guards. The long and the short of it was while Boston's St. Patrick's Day celebrations wound down, a pair of men dressed in the dark blue uniforms and service caps of city police officers gained entry to the museum's side entrance on Palace Road. More experienced—and alert—museum personnel might have asked them a few questions or followed the written security policy, which forbade unlocking the doors for any unknown person, but Kahn kept this opinion to himself. Second-guessing now was salt in the wound.

The detectives interviewed the two night guards separately. The twenty-three-year-old who unlocked the security doors wore his curly hair past his shoulders and Kahn's two neatly groomed younger detectives rolled their eyes as he explained how he'd been on edge.

"First a fire alarm went off upstairs. I checked it out—nothing, except the strobe lights flashing like maniacs. Then—and this shit *never* happens here—an alarm went off in the carriage house. I took a walk out there and didn't see anything, but it's dark and I can't be a hundred percent sure no one was hiding in the bushes or someplace." His hands twisted in his lap. "All these alarms gave me the creeps."

"And then?" Kahn prodded.

"Then these two cops show up. They said there was some kind of disturbance in the courtyard and they needed to investigate. And, I thought, 'Shit, yeah, I could use some backup here.' So I let them in."

Once inside, the fake police continued to display convincing authority, maintaining control over the situation. They ordered the guard out from behind the desk where he could have access to the museum's only external alarm button. They handcuffed him and when the other guard on duty appeared, they handcuffed him, too. In short order the guards were in the basement, bound hand and foot, their heads wrapped in duct tape, handcuffed to pipes some distance apart. Hours later, a guard from the day shift found them.

"Have you been a museum guard long?" Kahn asked.

"A while."

"This your only job?"

"I told you. I'm at Berklee." Berklee College of Music.

"And that's it?"

"I'm in a band and we play gigs around town."

"On nights you're not working or…?"

"No, I can get to the museum after."

"Do you ever come to work drunk? Or after a few beers?"

The young man glanced at the other detectives, then out the door. "No way."

"Stoned?"

Now he squirmed in the chair. "Once or twice."

"Were you drunk or stoned last night?"

"No, man. I was at the performance lab until late. You can check."

The note a detective made suggested they would.

"Anyway," the guard continued, "the Irish bands had all the gigs last night." He tossed his head and his long hair rearranged itself behind his shoulders.

The second guard added little and when these interviews were over, Kahn turned to his detectives. "Well?"

"Not real Boston cops," one said. "Too organized."

"I'd say mafia. Some low-level mopes just starting out," another said.

Kahn reflected. "Shouldn't we consider other possibilities? Mafia's too easy."

"That's what the FBI will focus on," the first detective said. "That's their hammer."

"Their hammer?" the other one said in a what-the-hell tone.

"To a hammer, everything's a nail. Mafia. That's their hammer."

"And here they come," Kahn said, pointing toward the door where six men in suits strode in.

The museum's security system recording revealed the thieves entered at 1:24 a.m. and stayed inside for eighty-one minutes. They made two trips to their vehicle with the loot and on their way out, they snatched the videotape for the side-door camera. The physical evidence Kahn and his men observed indicated that rather than carry the largest paintings out in their frames, some of which were several feet on a side, they cut them away, leaving behind broken glass and shredded canvas.

"Look what a mess they made," a curator said.

"Pretty good job, though, for men probably wearing gloves," Kahn said.

"What I don't understand," she said, "is why they took what they did. Some of the works they stole—like the two Degas drawings—are not particularly valuable. Relatively speaking. And yet they left other works worth so much more, including the Titian, the *Europa*." She snorted, thinking of it. *The Rape of Europa* was art-world shorthand for the looting of artworks in Nazi-occupied countries and now the plunderers struck here in Isabella Gardner's beautiful sanctuary. Under her breath she said, "Rape. Exactly what it feels like."

She wasn't the last to point out the odd assortment of targets, which led the FBI and other authorities to conclude the thieves were amateurs who didn't know what they were doing.

⚹   ⚹   ⚹   ⚹

Rome, Autumn, 1989

Some months before this record-shattering theft, Amit Madoor received a significant visitor at his Rome shop. The woman handed him a postcard-sized guide to the Isabella Stewart Gardner Museum that she'd brought from Boston. "You'd love it. The museum looks like a Renaissance Venetian palace," she said. "So elegant, yet informal. Like someone's home."

"Interesting." Madoor accepted the guide, intrigued by the implications of "informal."

"The painting on the front is Isabella Gardner herself in Venice. Isn't it lovely?"

"Indeed. She looks like a bird about to take flight." Madoor turned the small guide's pages, which described the museum's most important holdings and where the visitor would find them. He flipped back and forth to the floor plan inside the front cover.

"Keep it. I have no plans to return to the U.S.," his friend said.

"May I?" Madoor clutched the guide in both hands as if it were as precious as the objects it described. "It is really quite remarkable."

✗ ✗ ✗ ✗

Amit Madoor's antiquities shop on the Via in Selci—a narrow curving one-way Roman street between the Colosseum and the Basilica di Santa Maria Maggiore—attracted foot traffic from the western corner near the Cavour Metro station and the piazza at the eastern end, where five streets jumbled together. Yet it was not so near the main tourist attractions nor so elegant as to be in the high-rent district.

For some days after Madoor received the Gardner museum guide, tourists attracted to the shop window encountered a discreet "Closed" sign. Inside, Madoor was fully occupied with a series of lengthy long-distance telephone calls. Telephone security concerns being what they are in Italy, he took great care not to say directly what his business was. The people on the other end of the line whom his father recommended were quick and cooperative, even eager, once they understood his proposition and his guarantees.

They probably would not have understood the situation this way, but Madoor was turning the role of "fence" on its head, representing them—the buyers—in the world of gray-to-black art commerce, letting them create his shopping list. Madoor knew as well as anyone that stealing valuable artworks is child's play compared to disposing of them afterwards. By assuring the market was there before a theft, he dramatically reduced its downside risks. *If* he could find people brazen enough to carry it off.

✗ ✗ ✗ ✗

Fez, Morocco, the 1970s

His father's stall could be found deep in the medina, squeezed between a seller of a thousand brilliant colors of thread and a dentist whose painted sign bore a smile with an improbable number of teeth. Standing outside the stall, 13-year-old Amit Madoor greeted customers from all over the world. The shop sold silver rings and bracelets, but what made the family's fortune were the other services his father provided. These were discussed in a back room and perhaps it was the smoke and fumes from the nearby ironworkers' stalls that brought tears to the customers' eyes.

Did a man need a passport in another name? An entry visa? More important, sometimes, an exit visa? Permission to travel? Did a woman seek the name of a border official who could be bribed? Men pushed wrinkled documents and envelopes stuffed with money across the table; women held out velvet pouches heavy with jewelry.

At least for a time, his father was the most important person in the world to these people. As he worked out what would be needed, Amit saw the light return to their eyes. Negotiations concluded, his older brother—Rashid's father—would take customers by the arm and escort them through the dark and crowded passageways. Their steps became surer, their backs straighter as his brother walked them to safety.

These customers were former confidants of the Shah of Iran, supported Nasser in Egypt or rapacious governments anywhere in the developing world. They stole public money and lucrative corporate secrets, escaping disaster by sheer luck or because governments changed hands, or their replacements didn't want to risk exposure of their own dirty dealings. Over the years, the customers' politics and crimes changed, but not their desperation. In the world parade of bloody regimes and criminal conspiracies they found themselves on the wrong side of the street. Yet through attenuated family connections or relationships established in dusty trading posts or a friend of a friend of a friend, they ended up at a particular stall in the Fez medina.

One night, as they were closing the shop, Amit asked his father why he did what he did. "That man just here, that Javier Julima," Amit said, "he is very bad. Why do you help people like that?"

His father stopped his evening tasks to take his son's chin in his hand and said, "It is not up to me to judge a man's whole lifetime, the part that is to come. Think, Amit. If I sent him away without help, he would be killed within a week. He would die with all his sins on his heart and no chance to redeem himself. Our family gave him that chance and he may yet do some good in the world." As he spoke, Amit's father emptied the shop's cash register, putting the money in a zipper-bag he hid inside his *djellaba*.

"But will he?" Amit picked up the bag of oranges they were taking home to his mother and went to stand outside the shop while his father rolled down the overhead door and locked it.

"Some do. And, as long as they are alive, they have that opportunity. But if they do not, then I do not feel bad having taken their money. That does some good right here at home. Either way, there is a seed of good in what we do."

He put his arm around his son's shoulders and they walked home together. As they entered the house, his father put a coda on his reflections, saying, "No matter what path you follow in life, Amit, keep that seed alive. Even if you must do some bad thing, sweeten your act with good."

✗ ✗ ✗ ✗

Copley Plaza, Boston, March 18, 1990, 6 p.m.

Madoor watched television as he ate another room-service dinner in his hotel. The story of the unthinkable robbery at the Isabella Stewart Gardner Museum led the evening news. He saw the museum's director plead for the return of the stolen artworks. When she said they might be damaged if not properly cared for, he stabbed his fork at her. As if he wouldn't protect his investment. His father's investment!

Boston's chief of police came on screen, confident of an early close to the case, but was metaphorically if not literally elbowed aside by the head of the local FBI office. They were searching strenuously for fingerprints. Madoor rolled his eyes. They were checking their organized crime database and investigating the whereabouts of known art thieves. Madoor sighed. Even looking internationally. He raised an eyebrow, then returned attention to his lamb chops.

The museum director reappeared to narrate a hastily assembled slide show of the stolen works. There they were again—the three Rembrandts (*too bad no one requested that other self-portrait, he muttered, what a lost opportunity!*), the Vermeer, the Manet, the Flinck (for many years thought to be another Rembrandt, the director said), the ancient Chinese bronze, the eagle from atop a

Napoleonic banner (*the emperor's descendant will be disappointed we cannot provide the banner itself*) and five Degas drawings.

His fork clattered to his plate when among the Degas slides appeared not just the three drawings with horses, requested by a client trying to replicate an English country house in the Lebanese mountains, but also two studies called "Program for an Artistic Soirée." These drawings weren't on Madoor's list and they weren't in the cache Jack and Isaac delivered to him. He peered at the television.

Madoor finished the chops and started his salad as the nightly news drifted to more mundane matters: an impending City Council flap, another environmental roadblock in planning the Big Dig, and the strangulation murder of an auto upholstery repair shop owner. In broken English, the man's distraught wife said a rush job kept her husband working through the night. That was all she knew.

Madoor was pleased she followed the script on the note he left her, accompanied by an envelope thick with cash. She added only, "He was an artist," with unintended irony. Madoor shook his head sadly.

In the background of this footage, filmed outside the workshop where the body was found, stretched a row of grimy ramshackle buildings, their rolling doors shut tight. These spaces predominantly housed dodgy auto parts businesses—thinly disguised chop-shops—and both for practical reasons and out of long habit, their mostly immigrant owners avoided the police. Even if they possessed information, they wouldn't share it and, anyway, there was no reason for them to mention the two pristine 1950s Cadillacs momentarily parked in their alley the evening before.

Madoor sensed indifference ran both ways and the death of the Algerian upholsterer would fade quickly from official attention. As the anchorwoman's capsule news summary reminded viewers, the Boston police had bigger fish to fry.

He switched off the television. They'd done it. He closed his eyes and let the enormity of the accomplishment fill him. Until he saw the museum director on television and the B-roll of the empty places on the Gardner's jacquarded walls, the theft didn't seem quite real.

In memory the events of the night before appeared as a sequence of separate scenes that began when the surgical residents appeared out of the darkness and transferred the rolled-up paintings and other objects to the trunk of his rental car.

"We threw the plastic badges away," Jack said. "The toy guns, too. No place close to where we live. We'll red-bag the costumes in the morning."

"Red bag?" Madoor asked.

"They'll be on their way to the incinerator by noon. Nobody's going to root around in bags of medical waste," Isaac said.

In the next scene, Madoor stood in the shop smelling of leather and new vinyl admiring the Cadillacs. As the upholsterer sewed the artworks into the seat cushions, Madoor repeated his silent promise to take care of the man's family.

He relived the night's most difficult moment, the one that led to the body crumpled on the shop floor staring into eternal nothingness.

He saw the parking lot a few blocks away from the shop where he drove first one and then the other Cadillac and waited for Rashid to arrive. And finally, he recalled the activity on the dock as the Evergreen container was loaded, sealed and put aboard the ship.

Now he planned to stay here in his hotel until the *Annamarie* sailed. Once she was out of the harbor, he would fly to JFK and be on the next Rome-bound plane. He picked up his book and read one or two more pages, but the mystery of the Degas drawings kept creeping into his thoughts. They were quite similar, and he could picture them on the walls of two successful surgeons on opposite coasts, reminders of their great escapade and their ongoing mutual need to keep quiet. In the unlikely event anyone asked about them, they could say, "Reproductions. Not bad, though." It was the response people would expect, surely.

But just as likely, he could imagine the drawings were a false clue, a police trap for the inevitable ransom-seekers. Taking these two minor pieces off display would be a small sacrifice for the Gardner, compared to what was truly lost.

✗   ✗   ✗   ✗

Monday morning, a bored African-American woman brought Madoor's room service breakfast and the newspaper. Like everyone else at the hotel, she never connected this quiet guest with the *Globe*'s lurid headlines.

Around noon, Jack called. "Just wanted you to know. Those accounts you set up for Isaac and me seem to be working. I just paid off one of my loans, the smallest one."

"Your money is all there. But remember, you will want to spend only a little at a time for now."

"Got it. And we'll remember to keep complaining about our finances, too. Old habits are hard to break. I didn't realize..." Jack paused. "When I could finally pay that loan off, it meant a lot, really. It was like, I don't know, freedom, or..."

Madoor coughed and Jack said, "Isaac and I are taking your advice. We're looking forward, not back."

"That is best."

These two doctors both would have successful careers. They would never commit another such robbery. They would never be arrested for some crime and inveigled to trade freedom for information and they would never ever confess to a loose-lipped cellmate or prison stoolie. They would fly stratospheres above suspicion for their entire lives.

"One bit of advice, though," Jack said. "A box-cutter is a piss-poor tool. Makes a crappy cut. Not what I'm used to."

"Hmmm," Madoor acknowledged. "Best of luck to you, Dr. Jack. To you and Isaac. In your careers you will help many, many people. I'm glad to have helped you get your start. Now, be content and do good."

"We will. Thank you."

And enjoy your Degas. If you have them.

✗   ✗   ✗   ✗

Conley Terminal, Boston, Tuesday, March 20, noon

Madoor stood outside the terminal's chain-link fence. The *Annamarie*'s smokestack loosed a puff of black smoke, the ship shuddered and it glided away from the dock to join the traffic in Boston Harbor. He raised his hand in salute to the ship, its hundreds of shipping containers, the two Cadillacs and the priceless haul from history's largest property theft.

✗

Three of Victoria Weisfeld's short stories have appeared in *Ellery Queen's Mystery Magazine*; her story "Breadcrumbs," which appeared in *Betty Fedora*, Issue 3, won a 2017 Derringer Award; and her stories have appeared in the anthologies *Busted: Arresting Stories from the Beat*, *Murder Among Friends*, Bouchercon 2017's *Passport to Murder*, and *Quoth the Raven*, contemporary stories inspired by the works of Edgar Allan Poe. She has an active website (vweisfeld.com) designed to help readers sort through today's incredible array of book, theater, and movie choices. Authors will find tips on the writer's craft, and travelers may discover new destinations. She's a reviewer for crimefictionlover.com and TheFrontRowCenter.com. In rare moments when she's not writing, you may find her dancing or researching family history or baking a pie.

THE ADVENTURE OF WISTERIA LODGE

by Sir Arthur Conan Doyle

1. THE SINGULAR EXPERIENCE OF MR JOHN SCOTT ECCLES

I find it recorded in my notebook that it was a bleak and windy day towards the end of March in the year 1892. Holmes had received a telegram while we sat at our lunch, and he had scribbled a reply. He made no remark, but the matter remained in his thoughts, for he stood in front of the fire afterwards with a thoughtful face, smoking his pipe, and casting an occasional glance at the message. Suddenly he turned upon me with a mischievous twinkle in his eyes.

"I suppose, Watson, we must look upon you as a man of letters," said he. "How do you define the word 'grotesque'?"

"Strange—remarkable," I suggested.

He shook his head at my definition.

"There is surely something more than that," said he; "some underlying suggestion of the tragic and the terrible. If you cast your mind back to some of those narratives with which you have afflicted a long-suffering public, you will recognise how often the grotesque has deepened into the criminal. Think of that little affair of the red-headed men. That was grotesque enough in the outset, and yet it ended in a desperate attempt at robbery. Or, again, there was that most grotesque affair of the five orange pips, which led straight to a murderous conspiracy. The word puts me on the alert."

"Have you it there?" I asked.

He read the telegram aloud.

> Have just had most incredible and grotesque experience. May I consult you?
>
> SCOTT ECCLES,
> Post Office, Charing Cross.

"Man or woman?" I asked.

"Oh, man, of course. No woman would ever send a reply-paid telegram. She would have come."

"Will you see him?"

"My dear Watson, you know how bored I have been since we locked up Colonel Carruthers. My mind is like a racing engine, tearing itself to pieces because it is not connected up with the work for which it was built. Life is commonplace, the papers are sterile; audacity and romance seem to have passed forever from the criminal world. Can you ask me, then, whether I am ready to look into any new problem, however trivial it may prove? But here, unless I am mistaken, is our client."

A measured step was heard upon the stairs, and a moment later a stout, tall, grey-whiskered and solemnly respectable person was ushered into the room. His life history was written in his heavy features and pompous manner. From his spats to his gold-rimmed spectacles he was a Conservative, a churchman, a good citizen, orthodox and conventional to the last degree. But some amazing experience had disturbed his native composure and left its traces in his bristling hair, his flushed, angry cheeks, and his flurried, excited manner. He plunged instantly into his business.

"I have had a most singular and unpleasant experience, Mr Holmes," said he. "Never in my life have I been placed in such a situation. It is most improper—most outrageous. I must insist upon some explanation." He swelled and puffed in his anger.

"Pray sit down, Mr Scott Eccles," said Holmes in a soothing voice. "May I ask, in the first place, why you came to me at all?"

"Well, sir, it did not appear to be a matter which concerned the police, and yet, when you have heard the facts, you must admit that I could not leave it where it was. Private detectives are a class with whom I have absolutely no sympathy, but none the less, having heard your name—"

"Quite so. But, in the second place, why did you not come at once?"

Holmes glanced at his watch.

"It is a quarter-past two," he said. "Your telegram was dispatched about one. But no one can glance at your toilet and attire without seeing that your disturbance dates from the moment of your waking."

Our client smoothed down his unbrushed hair and felt his unshaven chin.

"You are right, Mr Holmes. I never gave a thought to my toilet. I was only too glad to get out of such a house. But I have been running round making inquiries before I came to you. I went to the house agents, you know, and they said that Mr Garcia's rent was paid up all right and that everything was in order at Wisteria Lodge."

"Come, come, sir," said Holmes, laughing. "You are like my friend, Dr Watson, who has a bad habit of telling his stories wrong end foremost. Please arrange your thoughts and let me know, in their due sequence, exactly what those events are which have sent you out unbrushed and unkempt, with dress boots and waistcoat buttoned awry, in search of advice and assistance."

Our client looked down with a rueful face at his own unconventional appearance.

"I'm sure it must look very bad, Mr Holmes, and I am not aware that in my whole life such a thing has ever happened before. But I will tell you the whole queer business, and when I have done so you will admit, I am sure, that there has been enough to excuse me."

But his narrative was nipped in the bud. There was a bustle outside, and Mrs Hudson opened the door to usher in two robust and official-looking individuals, one of whom was well known to us as Inspector Gregson of Scotland Yard, an energetic, gallant, and, within his limitations, a capable officer. He shook hands with Holmes and introduced his comrade as Inspector Baynes, of the Surrey Constabulary.

"We are hunting together, Mr Holmes, and our trail lay in this direction." He turned his bulldog eyes upon our visitor. "Are you Mr John Scott Eccles, of Popham House, Lee?"

"I am."

"We have been following you about all the morning."

"You traced him through the telegram, no doubt," said Holmes.

"Exactly, Mr Holmes. We picked up the scent at Charing Cross Post-Office and came on here."

"But why do you follow me? What do you want?"

"We wish a statement, Mr Scott Eccles, as to the events which led up to the death last night of Mr Aloysius Garcia, of Wisteria Lodge, near Esher."

Our client had sat up with staring eyes and every tinge of colour struck from his astonished face.

"Dead? Did you say he was dead?"

"Yes, sir, he is dead."

"But how? An accident?"

"Murder, if ever there was one upon earth."

"Good God! This is awful! You don't mean—you don't mean that I am suspected?"

"A letter of yours was found in the dead man's pocket, and we know by it that you had planned to pass last night at his house."

"So I did."

"Oh, you did, did you?"

Out came the official notebook.

"Wait a bit, Gregson," said Sherlock Holmes. "All you desire is a plain statement, is it not?"

"And it is my duty to warn Mr Scott Eccles that it may be used against him."

"Mr Eccles was going to tell us about it when you entered the room. I think, Watson, a brandy and soda would do him no harm. Now, sir, I suggest that you take no notice of this addition to your audience, and that you proceed with your narrative exactly as you would have done had you never been interrupted."

Our visitor had gulped off the brandy and the colour had returned to his face. With a dubious glance at the inspector's notebook, he plunged at once into his extraordinary statement.

"I am a bachelor," said he, "and being of a sociable turn I cultivate a large number of friends. Among these are the family of a retired brewer called Melville, living at Abermarle Mansion, Kensington. It was at his table that I met some weeks ago a young fellow named Garcia. He was, I understood, of Spanish descent and connected in some way with the embassy. He spoke perfect English, was pleasing in his manners, and as good-looking a man as ever I saw in my life.

"In some way we struck up quite a friendship, this young fellow and I. He seemed to take a fancy to me from the first, and within two days of our meeting he came to see me at Lee. One thing led to another, and it ended in his inviting me out to spend a few days at his house, Wisteria Lodge, between Esher and Oxshott. Yesterday evening I went to Esher to fulfil this engagement.

"He had described his household to me before I went there. He lived with a faithful servant, a countryman of his own, who looked after all his needs. This fellow could speak English and did his housekeeping for him. Then there was a wonderful cook, he said, a half-breed whom he had picked up in his travels, who could serve an excellent dinner. I remember that he remarked what a queer household it was to find in the heart of Surrey, and that I agreed with him, though it has proved a good deal queerer than I thought.

"I drove to the place—about two miles on the south side of Esher. The house was a fair-sized one, standing back from the road, with a curving drive which was banked with high evergreen shrubs. It was an old, tumbledown building in a crazy state of dis-repair. When the trap pulled up on the grass-grown drive in front of the blotched and weather-stained door, I had doubts as to my wisdom in visiting a man whom I knew so slightly. He opened the door himself, however, and greeted me with a great show of cordi-ality. I was handed over to the manservant, a melancholy, swarthy individual, who led the way, my bag in his hand, to my bedroom. The whole place was depressing. Our dinner was *tête-à-tête*, and though my host did his best to be entertaining, his thoughts seemed to continually wander, and he talked so vaguely and wildly that I could hardly understand him. He continually drummed his fingers on the table, gnawed his nails, and gave other signs of nervous impatience. The dinner itself was neither well served nor well cooked, and the gloomy presence of the taciturn servant did not help to enliven us. I can assure you that many times in the course of the evening I wished that I could invent some excuse which would take me back to Lee.

"One thing comes back to my memory which may have a bear-ing upon the business that you two gentlemen are investigating. I thought nothing of it at the time. Near the end of dinner a note was handed in by the servant. I noticed that after my host had read it he seemed even more distrait and strange than before. He gave up all pretence at conversation and sat, smoking endless cigarettes, lost in his own thoughts, but he made no remark as to the contents. About eleven I was glad to go to bed. Some time later Garcia looked in at my door—the room was dark at the time—and asked me if I had rung. I said that I had not. He apologised for having disturbed me so late, saying that it was nearly one o'clock. I dropped off after this and slept soundly all night.

"And now I come to the amazing part of my tale. When I woke it was broad daylight. I glanced at my watch, and the time was nearly nine. I had particularly asked to be called at eight, so I was very much astonished at this forgetfulness. I sprang up and rang for the servant. There was no response. I rang again and again, with the same result. Then I came to the conclusion that the bell was out of order. I huddled on my clothes and hurried downstairs in an exceedingly bad temper to order some hot water. You can imagine my surprise when I found that there was no one there. I shouted in the hall. There was no answer. Then I ran from room to room. All were deserted. My host had shown me which was his bedroom the night before, so I knocked at the door. No reply. I turned the handle and walked in. The room was empty, and the bed had never been slept in. He had gone with the rest. The foreign host, the foreign footman, the foreign cook, all had vanished in the night! That was the end of my visit to Wisteria Lodge."

Sherlock Holmes was rubbing his hands and chuckling as he added this bizarre incident to his collection of strange episodes.

"Your experience is, so far as I know, perfectly unique," said he. "May I ask, sir, what you did then?"

"I was furious. My first idea was that I had been the victim of some absurd practical joke. I packed my things, banged the hall door behind me, and set off for Esher, with my bag in my hand. I called at Allan Brothers', the chief land agents in the village, and found that it was from this firm that the villa had been rented. It struck me that the whole proceeding could hardly be for the purpose of making a fool of me, and that the main object must be to get out of the rent. It is late in March, so quarter-day is at hand. But this theory would not work. The agent was obliged to me for my warning, but told me that the rent had been paid in advance. Then I made my way to town and called at the Spanish embassy. The man was unknown there. After this I went to see Melville, at whose house I had first met Garcia, but I found that he really knew rather less about him than I did. Finally when I got your reply to my wire I came out to you, since I gather that you are a person who gives advice in difficult cases. But now, Mr Inspector, I understand, from what you said when you entered the room, that you can carry the story on, and that some tragedy had occurred. I can assure you that every word I have said is the truth, and that, outside of what I have told you, I know absolutely nothing about the fate of this man. My only desire is to help the law in every possible way."

"I am sure of it, Mr Scott Eccles—I am sure of it," said Inspector Gregson in a very amiable tone. "I am bound to say that everything which you have said agrees very closely with the facts as they have come to our notice. For example, there was that note which arrived during dinner. Did you chance to observe what became of it?"

"Yes, I did. Garcia rolled it up and threw it into the fire."

"What do you say to that, Mr Baynes?"

The country detective was a stout, puffy, red man, whose face was only redeemed from grossness by two extraordinarily bright eyes, almost hidden behind the heavy creases of cheek and brow. With a slow smile he drew a folded and discoloured scrap of paper from his pocket.

"It was a dog-grate, Mr Holmes, and he overpitched it. I picked this out unburned from the back of it."

Holmes smiled his appreciation.

"You must have examined the house very carefully to find a single pellet of paper."

"I did, Mr Holmes. It's my way. Shall I read it, Mr Gregson?"

The Londoner nodded.

"The note is written upon ordinary cream-laid paper without watermark. It is a quarter-sheet. The paper is cut off in two snips with a short-bladed scissors. It has been folded over three times and sealed with purple wax, put on hurriedly and pressed down with some flat oval object. It is addressed to Mr Garcia, Wisteria Lodge. It says:

"Our own colours, green and white. Green open, white shut. Main stair, first corridor, seventh right, green baize. Godspeed. D.

"It is a woman's writing, done with a sharp-pointed pen, but the address is either done with another pen or by someone else. It is thicker and bolder, as you see."

"A very remarkable note," said Holmes, glancing it over. "I must compliment you, Mr Baynes, upon your attention to detail in your examination of it. A few trifling points might perhaps be added. The oval seal is undoubtedly a plain sleeve-link—what else is of such a shape? The scissors were bent nail scissors. Short as the two snips are, you can distinctly see the same slight curve in each."

The country detective chuckled.

"I thought I had squeezed all the juice out of it, but I see there was a little over," he said. "I'm bound to say that I make nothing of the note except that there was something on hand, and that a woman, as usual, was at the bottom of it."

Mr Scott Eccles had fidgeted in his seat during this conversation.

"I am glad you found the note, since it corroborates my story," said he. "But I beg to point out that I have not yet heard what has happened to Mr Garcia, nor what has become of his household."

"As to Garcia," said Gregson, "that is easily answered. He was found dead this morning upon Oxshott Common, nearly a mile from his home. His head had been smashed to pulp by heavy blows of a sandbag or some such instrument, which had crushed rather than wounded. It is a lonely corner, and there is no house within a quarter of a mile of the spot. He had apparently been struck down first from behind, but his assailant had gone on beating him long after he was dead. It was a most furious assault. There are no footsteps nor any clue to the criminals."

"Robbed?"

"No, there was no attempt at robbery."

"This is very painful—very painful and terrible," said Mr Scott Eccles in a querulous voice, "but it is really uncommonly hard on me. I had nothing to do with my host going off upon a nocturnal excursion and meeting so sad an end. How do I come to be mixed up with the case?"

"Very simply, sir," Inspector Baynes answered. "The only document found in the pocket of the deceased was a letter from you saying that you would be with him on the night of his death. It was the envelope of this letter which gave us the dead man's name and address. It was after nine this morning when we reached his house and found neither you nor anyone else inside it. I wired to

Mr Gregson to run you down in London while I examined Wisteria Lodge. Then I came into town, joined Mr Gregson, and here we are."

"I think now," said Gregson, rising, "we had best put this matter into an official shape. You will come round with us to the station, Mr Scott Eccles, and let us have your statement in writing."

"Certainly, I will come at once. But I retain your services, Mr Holmes. I desire you to spare no expense and no pains to get at the truth."

My friend turned to the country inspector.

"I suppose that you have no objection sir to my collaborating with you, Mr Baynes?"

"Highly honoured, sir, I am sure."

"You appear to have been very prompt and businesslike in all that you have done. Was there any clue, may I ask, as to the exact hour that the man met his death?"

"He had been there since one o'clock. There was rain about that time, and his death had certainly been before the rain."

"But that is perfectly impossible, Mr Baynes," cried our client. "His voice is unmistakable. I could swear to it that it was he who addressed me in my bedroom at that very hour."

"Remarkable, but by no means impossible," said Holmes, smiling.

"You have a clue?" asked Gregson.

"On the face of it the case is not a very complex one, though it certainly presents some novel and interesting features. A further knowledge of facts is necessary before I would venture to give a final and definite opinion. By the way, Mr Baynes, did you find anything remarkable besides this note in your examination of the house?"

The detective looked at my friend in a singular way.

"There were," said he, "one or two *very* remarkable things. Perhaps when I have finished at the police-station you would care to come out and give me your opinion of them."

"I am entirely at your service," said Sherlock Holmes, ringing the bell. "You will show these gentlemen out, Mrs Hudson, and kindly send the boy with this telegram. He is to pay a five-shilling reply."

We sat for some time in silence after our visitors had left. Holmes smoked hard, with his brows drawn down over his keen eyes, and his head thrust forward in the eager way characteristic of the man.

"Well, Watson," he asked, turning suddenly upon me, "what do you make of it?"

"I can make nothing of this mystification of Scott Eccles."

"But the crime?"

"Well, taken with the disappearance of the man's companions, I should say that they were in some way concerned in the murder and had fled from justice."

"That is certainly a possible point of view. On the face of it you must admit, however, that it is very strange that his two servants should have been in a conspiracy against him and should have attacked him on the one night when he had a guest. They had him alone at their mercy every other night in the week."

"Then why did they fly?"

"Quite so. Why did they fly? There is a big fact. Another big fact is the remarkable experience of our client, Scott Eccles. Now, my dear Watson, is it beyond the limits of human ingenuity to furnish an explanation which would cover both of these big facts? If it were one which would also admit of the mysterious note with its very curious phraseology, why, then it would be worth accepting as a temporary hypothesis. If the fresh facts which come to our knowledge all fit themselves into the scheme, then our hypothesis may gradually become a solution."

"But what is our hypothesis?"

Holmes leaned back in his chair with half-closed eyes.

"You must admit, my dear Watson, that the idea of a joke is impossible. There were grave events afoot, as the sequel showed, and the coaxing of Scott Eccles to Wisteria Lodge had some connection with them."

"But what possible connection?"

"Let us take it link by link. There is, on the face of it, something unnatural about this strange and sudden friendship between the young Spaniard and Scott Eccles. It was the former who forced the pace. He called upon Eccles at the other end of London on the very day after he first met him, and he kept in close touch with him until he got him down to Esher. Now, what did he want with

Eccles? What could Eccles supply? I see no charm in the man. He is not particularly intelligent—not a man likely to be congenial to a quick-witted Latin. Why, then, was he picked out from all the other people whom Garcia met as particularly suited to his purpose? Has he any one outstanding quality? I say that he has. He is the very type of conventional British respectability, and the very man as a witness to impress another Briton. You saw yourself how neither of the inspectors dreamed of questioning his statement, extraordinary as it was."

"But what was he to witness?"

"Nothing, as things turned out, but everything had they gone another way. That is how I read the matter."

"I see, he might have proved an alibi."

"Exactly, my dear Watson; he might have proved an alibi. We will suppose, for argument's sake, that the household of Wisteria Lodge are confederates in some design. The attempt, whatever it may be, is to come off, we will say, before one o'clock. By some juggling of the clocks it is quite possible that they may have got Scott Eccles to bed earlier than he thought, but in any case it is likely that when Garcia went out of his way to tell him that it was one it was really not more than twelve. If Garcia could do whatever he had to do and be back by the hour mentioned he had evidently a powerful reply to any accusation. Here was this irreproachable Englishman ready to swear in any court of law that the accused was in the house all the time. It was an insurance against the worst."

"Yes, yes, I see that. But how about the disappearance of the others?"

"I have not all my facts yet, but I do not think there are any insuperable difficulties. Still, it is an error to argue in front of your data. You find yourself insensibly twisting them round to fit your theories."

"And the message?"

"How did it run? 'Our own colours, green and white.' Sounds like racing. 'Green open, white shut.' That is clearly a signal. 'Main stair, first corridor, seventh right, green baize.' This is an assignation. We may find a jealous husband at the bottom of it all. It was clearly a dangerous quest. She would not have said 'Godspeed' had it not been so. 'D'—that should be a guide."

"The man was a Spaniard. I suggest that 'D' stands for Dolores, a common female name in Spain."

"Good, Watson, very good—but quite inadmissible. A Spaniard would write to a Spaniard in Spanish. The writer of this note is certainly English. Well, we can only possess our soul in patience until this excellent inspector comes back for us. Meanwhile we can thank our lucky fate which has rescued us for a few short hours from the insufferable fatigues of idleness."

⚹   ⚹   ⚹   ⚹

An answer had arrived to Holmes's telegram before our Surrey officer had returned. Holmes read it and was about to place it in his notebook when he caught a glimpse of my expectant face. He tossed it across with a laugh.

"We are moving in exalted circles," said he.

The telegram was a list of names and addresses:

Lord Harringby, The Dingle; Sir George Ffolliott, Oxshott Towers; Mr Hynes Hynes, J.P., Purdley Place; Mr James Baker Williams, Forton Old Hall; Mr Henderson, High Gable; Rev Joshua Stone, Nether Walsling.

"This is a very obvious way of limiting our field of operations," said Holmes. "No doubt Baynes, with his methodical mind, has already adopted some similar plan."

"I don't quite understand."

"Well, my dear fellow, we have already arrived at the conclusion that the message received by Garcia at dinner was an appointment or an assignation. Now if the obvious reading of it is correct and in order to keep the tryst one has to ascend a main stair and seek the seventh door in a corridor, it is perfectly clear that the house is a very large one. It is equally certain that this house cannot be more than a mile or two from Oxshott since Garcia was walking in that direction and hoped, according to my reading of the facts, to be back in Wisteria Lodge in time to avail himself of an alibi, which would only be valid up to one o'clock. As the number of large houses close to Oxshott must be limited, I adopted the obvious method of sending to the agents mentioned by Scott Eccles and obtaining a list of them. Here they are in this telegram and the other end of our tangled skein must lie among them."

It was nearly six o'clock before we found ourselves in the pretty Surrey village of Esher, with Inspector Baynes as our companion.

Holmes and I had taken things for the night and found comfortable quarters at the Bull. Finally we set out in the company of the detective on our visit to Wisteria Lodge. It was a cold dark March evening with a sharp wind and a fine rain beating upon our faces, a fit setting for the wild common over which our road passed and the tragic goal to which it led us.

2. THE TIGER OF SAN PEDRO

A cold and melancholy walk of a couple of miles brought us to a high wooden gate, which opened into a gloomy avenue of chestnuts. The curved and shadowed drive led us to a low, dark house, pitch-black against a slate-coloured sky. From the front window upon the left of the door there peeped a glimmer of a feeble light.

"There's a constable in possession," said Baynes. "I'll knock at the window." He stepped across the grass plot and tapped with his hand on the pane. Through the fogged glass I dimly saw a man spring up from a chair beside the fire, and heard a sharp cry from within the room. An instant later a white-faced, hard-breathing policeman had opened the door, the candle wavering in his trembling hand.

"What's the matter, Walters?" asked Baynes sharply.

The man mopped his forehead with his handkerchief and gave a long sigh of relief.

"I am glad you have come, sir. It has been a long evening, and I don't think my nerve is as good as it was."

"Your nerve, Walters? I should not have thought you had a nerve in your body."

"Well, sir, it's this lonely, silent house and the queer thing in the kitchen. Then when you tapped at the window I thought it had come again."

"That what had come again?"

"The devil, sir, for all I know. It was at the window."

"What was at the window, and when?"

"It was just about two hours ago. The light was just fading. I was sitting reading in the chair. I don't know what made me look up, but there was a face looking in at me through the lower pane. Lord, sir, what a face it was! I'll see it in my dreams."

"Tut, tut, Walters. This is not talk for a police-constable."

"I know, sir, I know; but it shook me, sir, and there's no use to deny it. It wasn't black, sir, nor was it white, nor any colour that I know but a kind of queer shade like clay with a splash of milk in it. Then there was the size of it—it was twice yours, sir. And the look of it—the great staring goggle eyes, and the line of white teeth like a hungry beast. I tell you, sir, I couldn't move a finger, nor get my breath, till it whisked away and was gone. Out I ran and through the shrubbery, but thank God there was no one there."

"If I didn't know you were a good man, Walters, I should put a black mark against you for this. If it were the devil himself a constable on duty should never thank God that he could not lay his hands upon him. I suppose the whole thing is not a vision and a touch of nerves?"

"That, at least, is very easily settled," said Holmes, lighting his little pocket lantern. "Yes," he reported, after a short examination of the grass bed, "a number twelve shoe, I should say. If he was all on the same scale as his foot he must certainly have been a giant."

"What became of him?"

"He seems to have broken through the shrubbery and made for the road."

"Well," said the inspector with a grave and thoughtful face, "whoever he may have been, and whatever he may have wanted, he's gone for the present, and we have more immediate things to attend to. Now, Mr Holmes, with your permission, I will show you round the house."

The various bedrooms and sitting-rooms had yielded nothing to a careful search. Apparently the tenants had brought little or nothing with them, and all the furniture down to the smallest details had been taken over with the house. A good deal of clothing with the stamp of Marx and Co., High Holborn, had been left behind. Telegraphic inquiries had been already made which showed that Marx knew nothing of his customer save that he was a good payer. Odds and ends, some pipes, a few novels, two of them in Spanish, an old-fashioned pinfire revolver, and a guitar were among the personal property.

"Nothing in all this," said Baynes, stalking, candle in hand, from room to room. "But now, Mr Holmes, I invite your attention to the kitchen."

It was a gloomy, high-ceilinged room at the back of the house, with a straw litter in one corner, which served apparently as a bed for the cook. The table was piled with half-eaten dishes and dirty plates, the debris of last night's dinner.

"Look at this," said Baynes. "What do you make of it?"

He held up his candle before an extraordinary object which stood at the back of the dresser. It was so wrinkled and shrunken and withered that it was difficult to say what it might have been. One could but say that it was black and leathery and that it bore some resemblance to a dwarfish, human figure. At first, as I examined it, I thought that it was a mummified negro baby, and then it seemed a very twisted and ancient monkey. Finally I was left in doubt as to whether it was animal or human. A double band of white shells were strung round the centre of it.

"Very interesting—very interesting, indeed!" said Holmes, peering at this sinister relic. "Anything more?"

In silence Baynes led the way to the sink and held forward his candle. The limbs and body of some large, white bird, torn savagely to pieces with the feathers still on, were littered all over it. Holmes pointed to the wattles on the severed head.

"A white cock," said he. "Most interesting! It is really a very curious case."

But Mr Baynes had kept his most sinister exhibit to the last. From under the sink he drew a zinc pail which contained a quantity of blood. Then from the table he took a platter heaped with small pieces of charred bone.

"Something has been killed and something has been burned. We raked all these out of the fire. We had a doctor in this morning. He says that they are not human."

Holmes smiled and rubbed his hands.

"I must congratulate you, Inspector, on handling so distinctive and instructive a case. Your powers, if I may say so without offence, seem superior to your opportunities."

Inspector Baynes's small eyes twinkled with pleasure.

"You're right, Mr Holmes. We stagnate in the provinces. A case of this sort gives a man a chance, and I hope that I shall take it. What do you make of these bones?"

"A lamb, I should say, or a kid."

"And the white cock?"

"Curious, Mr Baynes, very curious. I should say almost unique."

"Yes, sir, there must have been some very strange people with some very strange ways in this house. One of them is dead. Did his companions follow him and kill him? If they did we should have them, for every port is watched. But my own views are different. Yes, sir, my own views are very different."

"You have a theory, then?"

"And I'll work it myself, Mr Holmes. It's only due to my own credit to do so. Your name is made, but I have still to make mine. I should be glad to be able to say afterwards that I had solved it without your help."

Holmes laughed good-humouredly.

"Well, well, Inspector," said he. "Do you follow your path and I will follow mine. My results are always very much at your service if you care to apply to me for them. I think that I have seen all that I wish in this house, and that my time may be more profitably employed elsewhere. *Au revoir* and good luck!"

I could tell by numerous subtle signs, which might have been lost upon anyone but myself, that Holmes was on a hot scent. As impassive as ever to the casual observer, there were none the less a subdued eagerness and suggestion of tension in his brightened eyes and brisker manner which assured me that the game was afoot. After his habit he said nothing, and after mine I asked no questions. Sufficient for me to share the sport and lend my humble help to the capture without distracting that intent brain with needless interruption. All would come round to me in due time.

I waited, therefore—but to my ever-deepening disappointment I waited in vain. Day succeeded day, and my friend took no step forward. One morning he spent in town, and I learned from a casual reference that he had visited the British Museum. Save for this one excursion, he spent his days in long and often solitary walks, or in chatting with a number of village gossips whose acquaintance he had cultivated.

"I'm sure, Watson, a week in the country will be invaluable to you," he remarked. "It is very pleasant to see the first green shoots upon the hedges and the catkins on the hazels once again. With a spud, a tin box, and an elementary book on botany, there are instructive days to be spent." He prowled about with this equipment himself, but it was a poor show of plants which he would bring back of an evening.

Occasionally in our rambles we came across Inspector Baynes. His fat, red face wreathed itself in smiles and his small eyes glittered as he greeted my companion. He said little about the case, but from that little we gathered that he also was not dissatisfied at the course of events. I must admit, however, that I was somewhat surprised when, some five days after the crime, I opened my morning paper to find in large letters:

THE OXSHOTT MYSTERY
A SOLUTION
ARREST OF SUPPOSED ASSASSIN

Holmes sprang in his chair as if he had been stung when I read the headlines.

"By Jove!" he cried. "You don't mean that Baynes has got him?"

"Apparently," said I as I read the following report:

Great excitement was caused in Esher and the neighbouring district when it was learned late last night that an arrest had been effected in connection with the Oxshott murder. It will be remembered that Mr Garcia, of Wisteria Lodge, was found dead on Oxshott Common, his body showing signs of extreme violence, and that on the same night his servant and his cook fled, which appeared to show their participation in the crime. It was suggested, but never proved, that the deceased gentleman may have had valuables in the house, and that their abstraction was the motive of the crime. Every effort was made by Inspector Baynes, who has the case in hand, to ascertain the hiding place of the fugitives, and he had good reason to believe that they had not gone far but were lurking in some retreat which had been already prepared. It was certain from the first, however, that they would eventually be detected, as the cook, from the evidence of one or two tradespeople who have caught a glimpse of him through the window, was a man of most remarkable appearance—being a huge and hideous mulatto, with yellowish features of a pronounced negroid type. This man has been seen since the crime, for he was detected and pursued by Constable Walters on the same evening, when he had the audacity to revisit Wisteria Lodge. Inspector Baynes, considering that such a visit must have some purpose in view and was likely, therefore, to be repeated, abandoned the house but left an ambuscade in the shrubbery. The man walked into the trap and was captured last night after a struggle in which Constable Downing was badly bitten by the savage. We understand that when the prisoner is brought before the magistrates a remand will be applied for by the police, and that great developments are hoped from his capture.

"Really we must see Baynes at once," cried Holmes, picking up his hat. "We will just catch him before he starts." We hurried down the village street and found, as we had expected, that the inspector was just leaving his lodgings.

"You've seen the paper, Mr Holmes?" he asked, holding one out to us.

"Yes, Baynes, I've seen it. Pray don't think it a liberty if I give you a word of friendly warning."

"Of warning, Mr Holmes?"

"I have looked into this case with some care, and I am not convinced that you are on the right lines. I don't want you to commit yourself too far unless you are sure."

"You're very kind, Mr Holmes."

"I assure you I speak for your good."

It seemed to me that something like a wink quivered for an instant over one of Mr Baynes's tiny eyes.

"We agreed to work on our own lines, Mr Holmes. That's what I am doing."

"Oh, very good," said Holmes. "Don't blame me."

"No, sir; I believe you mean well by me. But we all have our own systems, Mr Holmes. You have yours, and maybe I have mine."

"Let us say no more about it."

"You're welcome always to my news. This fellow is a perfect savage, as strong as a cart-horse and as fierce as the devil. He chewed Downing's thumb nearly off before they could master him.

He hardly speaks a word of English, and we can get nothing out of him but grunts."

"And you think you have evidence that he murdered his late master?"

"I didn't say so, Mr Holmes; I didn't say so. We all have our little ways. You try yours and I will try mine. That's the agreement."

Holmes shrugged his shoulders as we walked away together. "I can't make the man out. He seems to be riding for a fall. Well, as he says, we must each try our own way and see what comes of it. But there's something in Inspector Baynes which I can't quite understand."

"Just sit down in that chair, Watson," said Sherlock Holmes when we had returned to our apartment at the Bull. "I want to put you in touch with the situation, as I may need your help to-night. Let me show you the evolution of this case so far as I have been able to follow it. Simple as it has been in its leading features, it has none the less presented surprising difficulties in the way of an arrest. There are gaps in that direction which we have still to fill.

"We will go back to the note which was handed in to Garcia upon the evening of his death. We may put aside this idea of Baynes's that Garcia's servants were concerned in the matter. The proof of this lies in the fact that it was *he* who had arranged for the presence of Scott Eccles, which could only have been done for the purpose of an alibi. It was Garcia, then, who had an enterprise, and apparently a criminal enterprise, in hand that night in the course of which he met his death. I say 'criminal' because only a man with a criminal enterprise desires to establish an alibi. Who, then, is most likely to have taken his life? Surely the person against whom the criminal enterprise was directed. So far it seems to me that we are on safe ground.

"We can now see a reason for the disappearance of Garcia's household. They were *all* confederates in the same unknown crime. If it came off when Garcia returned, any possible suspicion would be warded off by the Englishman's evidence, and all would be well. But the attempt was a dangerous one, and if Garcia did *not* return by a certain hour it was probable that his own life had been sacrificed. It had been arranged, therefore, that in such a case his two subordinates were to make for some prearranged spot where they could escape investigation and be in a position afterwards to renew their attempt. That would fully explain the facts, would it not?"

The whole inexplicable tangle seemed to straighten out before me. I wondered, as I always did, how it had not been obvious to me before.

"But why should one servant return?"

"We can imagine that in the confusion of flight something precious, something which he could not bear to part with, had been left behind. That would explain his persistence, would it not?"

"Well, what is the next step?"

"The next step is the note received by Garcia at the dinner. It indicates a confederate at the other end. Now, where was the other end? I have already shown you that it could only lie in some large house, and that the number of large houses is limited. My first days in this village were devoted to a series of walks in which in the intervals of my botanical researches I made a reconnaissance of all the large houses and an examination of the family history of the occupants. One house, and only one, riveted my attention. It is the famous old Jacobean grange of High Gable, one mile on the farther side of Oxshott, and less than half a mile from the scene of the tragedy. The other mansions belonged to prosaic and respectable people who live far aloof from romance. But Mr Henderson, of High Gable, was by all accounts a curious man to whom curious adventures might befall. I concentrated my attention, therefore, upon him and his household.

"A singular set of people, Watson—the man himself the most singular of them all. I managed to see him on a plausible pretext, but I seemed to read in his dark, deepset, brooding eyes that he was perfectly aware of my true business. He is a man of fifty, strong, active, with iron-grey hair, great bunched black eyebrows, the step of a deer and the air of an emperor—a fierce, masterful man, with a red-hot spirit behind his parchment face. He is either a foreigner or has lived long in the tropics, for he is yellow and sapless, but tough as whipcord. His friend and secretary, Mr Lucas, is undoubtedly a foreigner, chocolate brown, wily, suave, and catlike, with a poisonous gentleness of speech. You see, Watson, we have come already upon two sets of foreigners—one at Wisteria Lodge and one at High Gable—so our gaps are beginning to close.

"These two men, close and confidential friends, are the centre of the household; but there is one other person who for our immediate purpose may be even more important. Henderson has two children—girls of eleven and thirteen. Their governess is a Miss Burnet, an Englishwoman of forty or thereabouts. There is also one confidential manservant. This little group forms the real family, for they travel about together, and Henderson is a great traveller, always on the move. It is only within the last weeks that he has returned, after a year's absence, to High Gable. I may add that he is enormously rich, and whatever his whims may be he can very easily satisfy them. For the rest, his house is full of butlers, footmen, maidservants, and the usual overfed, underworked staff of a large English country house.

"So much I learned partly from village gossip and partly from my own observation. There are no better instruments than discharged servants with a grievance, and I was lucky enough to find one. I call it luck, but it would not have come my way had I not been looking out for it. As Baynes remarks, we all have our systems. It was my system which enabled me to find John Warner, late gardener of High Gable, sacked in a moment of temper by his imperious employer. He in turn had friends among the indoor servants who unite in their fear and dislike of their master. So I had my key to the secrets of the establishment.

"Curious people, Watson! I don't pretend to understand it all yet, but very curious people anyway. It's a double-winged house, and the servants live on one side, the family on the other. There's no link between the two save for Henderson's own servant, who serves the family's meals. Everything is carried to a certain door, which forms the one connection. Governess and children hardly go out at all, except into the garden. Henderson never by any chance walks alone. His dark secretary is like his shadow. The gossip among the servants is that their master is terribly afraid of something. 'Sold his soul to the devil in exchange for money,' says Warner, 'and expects his creditor to come up and claim his own.' Where they came from, or who they are, nobody has an idea. They are very violent. Twice Henderson has lashed at folk with his dog-whip, and only his long purse and heavy compensation have kept him out of the courts.

"Well, now, Watson, let us judge the situation by this new information. We may take it that the letter came out of this strange household and was an invitation to Garcia to carry out some attempt which had already been planned. Who wrote the note? It was someone within the citadel, and it was a woman. Who then but Miss Burnet, the governess? All our reasoning seems to point that way. At any rate, we may take it as a hypothesis and see what consequences it would entail. I may add that Miss Burnet's age and character make it certain that my first idea that there might be a love interest in our story is out of the question.

"If she wrote the note she was presumably the friend and confederate of Garcia. What, then, might she be expected to do if she heard of his death? If he met it in some nefarious enterprise her lips might be sealed. Still, in her heart, she must retain bitterness and hatred against those who had killed him and would presumably help so far as she could to have revenge upon them. Could we see her, then and try to use her? That was my first thought. But now we come to a sinister fact. Miss Burnet has not been seen by any human eye since the night of the murder. From that evening she has utterly vanished. Is she alive? Has she perhaps met her end on the same night as the friend whom she had summoned? Or is she merely a prisoner? There is the point which we still have to decide.

"You will appreciate the difficulty of the situation, Watson. There is nothing upon which we can apply for a warrant. Our whole scheme might seem fantastic if laid before a magistrate. The woman's disappearance counts for nothing, since in that extraordinary household any member of it might be invisible for a week. And yet she may at the present moment be in danger of her life. All I can do is to watch the house and leave my agent, Warner, on guard at the gates. We can't let such a situation continue. If the law can do nothing we must take the risk ourselves."

"What do you suggest?"

"I know which is her room. It is accessible from the top of an outhouse. My suggestion is that you and I go to-night and see if we can strike at the very heart of the mystery."

It was not, I must confess, a very alluring prospect. The old house with its atmosphere of murder, the singular and formidable inhabitants, the unknown dangers of the approach, and the fact that we were putting ourselves legally in a false position all combined to damp my ardour. But there was something in the ice-cold reasoning of Holmes which made it impossible to shrink from any adventure which he might recommend. One knew that thus, and only thus, could a solution be found. I clasped his hand in silence, and the die was cast.

But it was not destined that our investigation should have so adventurous an ending. It was about five o'clock, and the shadows of the March evening were beginning to fall, when an excited rustic rushed into our room.

"They've gone, Mr Holmes. They went by the last train. The lady broke away, and I've got her in a cab downstairs."

"Excellent, Warner!" cried Holmes, springing to his feet. "Watson, the gaps are closing rapidly."

In the cab was a woman, half-collapsed from nervous exhaustion. She bore upon her aquiline and emaciated face the traces of some recent tragedy. Her head hung listlessly upon her breast, but as she raised it and turned her dull eyes upon us I saw that her pupils were dark dots in the centre of the broad grey iris. She was drugged with opium.

"I watched at the gate, same as you advised, Mr Holmes," said our emissary, the discharged gardener. "When the carriage came out I followed it to the station. She was like one walking in her sleep, but when they tried to get her into the train she came to life and struggled. They pushed her into the carriage. She fought her way out again. I took her part, got her into a cab, and here we are. I shan't forget the face at the carriage window as I led her away. I'd have a short life if he had his way—the black-eyed, scowling, yellow devil."

We carried her upstairs, laid her on the sofa, and a couple of cups of the strongest coffee soon cleared her brain from the mists of the drug. Baynes had been summoned by Holmes, and the situation rapidly explained to him.

"Why, sir, you've got me the very evidence I want," said the inspector warmly, shaking my friend by the hand. "I was on the same scent as you from the first."

"What! You were after Henderson?"

"Why, Mr. Holmes, when you were crawling in the shrubbery at High Gable I was up one of the trees in the plantation and saw you down below. It was just who would get his evidence first."

"Then why did you arrest the mulatto?"

Baynes chuckled.

"I was sure Henderson, as he calls himself, felt that he was suspected, and that he would lie low and make no move so long as he thought he was in any danger. I arrested the wrong man to make him believe that our eyes were off him. I knew he would be likely to clear off then and give us a chance of getting at Miss Burnet."

Holmes laid his hand upon the inspector's shoulder.

"You will rise high in your profession. You have instinct and intuition," said he.

Baynes flushed with pleasure.

"I've had a plain-clothes man waiting at the station all the week. Wherever the High Gable folk go he will keep them in sight. But he must have been hard put to it when Miss Burnet broke away. However, your man picked her up, and it all ends well. We can't arrest without her evidence, that is clear, so the sooner we get a statement the better."

"Every minute she gets stronger," said Holmes, glancing at the governess. "But tell me, Baynes, who is this man Henderson?"

"Henderson," the inspector answered, "is Don Murillo, once called the Tiger of San Pedro."

The Tiger of San Pedro! The whole history of the man came back to me in a flash. He had made his name as the most lewd and bloodthirsty tyrant that had ever governed any country with a pretence to civilisation. Strong, fearless, and energetic, he had sufficient virtue to enable him to impose his odious vices upon a cowering people for ten or twelve years. His name was a terror through all Central America. At the end of that time there was a universal rising against him. But he was as cunning as he was cruel, and at the first whisper of coming trouble he had secretly conveyed his treasures aboard a ship which was manned by devoted adherents. It was an empty palace which was stormed by the insurgents next day. The dictator, his two children, his secretary, and his wealth had all escaped them. From that moment he had vanished from the world, and his identity had been a frequent subject for comment in the European press.

"Yes, sir, Don Murillo, the Tiger of San Pedro," said Baynes. "If you look it up you will find that the San Pedro colours are green and white, same as in the note, Mr Holmes. Henderson he called himself, but I traced him back, Paris and Rome and Madrid to Barcelona, where his ship came in in '86. They've been looking for him all the time for their revenge, but it is only now that they have begun to find him out."

"They discovered him a year ago," said Miss Burnet, who had sat up and was now intently following the conversation. "Once already his life has been attempted, but some evil spirit shielded him. Now, again, it is the noble, chivalrous Garcia who has fallen, while the monster goes safe. But another will come, and yet another, until some day justice will be done; that is as certain as the rise of to-morrow's sun." Her thin hands clenched, and her worn face blanched with the passion of her hatred.

"But how come you into this matter, Miss Burnet?" asked Holmes. "How can an English lady join in such a murderous affair?"

"I join in it because there is no other way in the world by which justice can be gained. What does the law of England care for the rivers of blood shed years ago in San Pedro, or for the shipload of treasure which this man has stolen? To you they are like crimes committed in some other planet. But *we* know. We have learned the truth in sorrow and in suffering. To us there is no fiend in hell like Juan Murillo, and no peace in life while his victims still cry for vengeance."

"No doubt," said Holmes, "he was as you say. I have heard that he was atrocious. But how are you affected?"

"I will tell you it all. This villain's policy was to murder, on one pretext or another, every man who showed such promise that he might in time come to be a dangerous rival. My husband—yes, my real name is Signora Victor Durando—was the San Pedro minister in London. He met me and married me there. A nobler man never lived upon earth. Unhappily, Murillo heard of his excellence, recalled him on some pretext, and had him shot. With a premonition of his fate he had refused to take me with him. His estates were confiscated, and I was left with a pittance and a broken heart.

"Then came the downfall of the tyrant. He escaped as you have just described. But the many whose lives he had ruined, whose nearest and dearest had suffered torture and death at his hands, would not let the matter rest. They banded themselves into a society which should never be dissolved until the work was done. It was my part after we had discovered in the transformed Henderson the fallen despot, to attach myself to his household and keep the others in touch with his movements. This I was able to do by securing the position of governess in his family. He little knew that the woman who faced him at every meal was the woman whose husband he had hurried at an hour's notice into eternity. I smiled on him, did my duty to his children, and bided my time. An attempt was made in Paris and failed. We zig-zagged swiftly here and there over Europe to throw off the pursuers and finally returned to this house, which he had taken upon his first arrival in England.

"But here also the ministers of justice were waiting. Knowing that he would return there, Garcia, who is the son of the former highest dignitary in San Pedro, was waiting with two trusty companions of humble station, all three fired with the same reasons for revenge. He could do little during the day, for Murillo took every precaution and never went out save with his satellite Lucas, or Lopez as he was known in the days of his greatness. At night, however, he slept alone, and the avenger might find him. On a certain evening, which had been prearranged, I sent my friend final instructions, for the man was forever on the alert and continually changed his room. I was to see that the doors were open and the signal of a green or white light in a window which faced the drive was to give notice if all was safe or if the attempt had better be postponed.

"But everything went wrong with us. In some way I had excited the suspicion of Lopez, the secretary. He crept up behind me and sprang upon me just as I had finished the note. He and his master dragged me to my room and held judgment upon me as a convicted traitress. Then and there they would have plunged their knives into me could they have seen how to escape the consequences of the deed. Finally, after much debate, they concluded that my murder was too dangerous. But they determined to get rid forever of Garcia. They had gagged me, and Murillo twisted my arm round until I gave him the address. I swear that he might have twisted it off had I understood what it would mean to Garcia. Lopez addressed the note which I had written, sealed it with his sleeve-link, and sent it by the hand of the servant, Jose. How they murdered him I do not know, save that it was Murillo's hand who struck him down, for Lopez had remained to guard me. I believe he must have waited among the gorse bushes through which the path winds and struck him down as he passed. At first they were of a mind to let him enter the house and to kill him as a detected burglar; but they argued that if they were mixed up in an inquiry their own identity would at once be publicly disclosed and they would be open to further attacks. With the death of Garcia, the pursuit might cease, since such a death might frighten others from the task.

"All would now have been well for them had it not been for my knowledge of what they had done. I have no doubt that there were times when my life hung in the balance. I was confined to my room, terrorised by the most horrible threats, cruelly ill-used to break my spirit—see this stab on my shoulder and the bruises from end to end of my arms—and a gag was thrust into my mouth on the one occasion when I tried to call from the window. For five days this cruel imprisonment continued, with hardly enough food to hold body and soul together. This afternoon a good lunch was brought me, but the moment after I took it I knew that I had been drugged. In a sort of dream I remember being half-led, half-carried to the carriage; in the same state I was conveyed to the train. Only then, when the wheels were almost moving, did I suddenly realise that my liberty lay in my own hands. I sprang out, they tried to drag me back, and had it not been for the help of this good man, who led me to the cab, I should never had broken away. Now, thank God, I am beyond their power forever."

We had all listened intently to this remarkable statement. It was Holmes who broke the silence.

"Our difficulties are not over," he remarked, shaking his head. "Our police work ends, but our legal work begins."

"Exactly," said I. "A plausible lawyer could make it out as an act of self-defense. There may be a hundred crimes in the background, but it is only on this one that they can be tried."

"Come, come," said Baynes cheerily, "I think better of the law than that. Self-defense is one thing. To entice a man in cold blood with the object of murdering him is another, whatever danger you may fear from him. No, no, we shall all be justified when we see the tenants of High Gable at the next Guildford Assizes."

It is a matter of history, however, that a little time was still to elapse before the Tiger of San Pedro should meet with his deserts. Wily and bold, he and his companion threw their pursuer off their track by entering a lodging-house in Edmonton Street and leaving by the back-gate into Curzon Square. From that day they were seen no more in England. Some six months afterwards the Marquess of Montalva and Signor Rulli, his secretary, were both murdered in their rooms at the Hotel Escurial at Madrid. The crime was ascribed to Nihilism, and the murderers were never arrested. Inspector Baynes visited us at Baker Street with a printed description of the dark face of the secretary, and of the masterful features, the magnetic black eyes, and the tufted brows of his master. We could not doubt that justice, if belated, had come at last.

"A chaotic case, my dear Watson," said Holmes over an evening pipe. "It will not be possible for you to present in that compact form which is dear to your heart. It covers two continents, concerns two groups of mysterious persons, and is further complicated by the highly respectable presence of our friend, Scott Eccles, whose inclusion shows me that the deceased Garcia had a scheming mind and a well-developed instinct of self-preservation. It is remarkable only for the fact that amid a perfect jungle of possibilities we, with our worthy collaborator, the inspector, have kept our close hold on the essentials and so been guided along the crooked and winding path. Is there any point which is not quite clear to you?"

"The object of the mulatto cook's return?"

"I think that the strange creature in the kitchen may account for it. The man was a primitive savage from the backwoods of San Pedro, and this was his fetish. When his companion and he had fled to some prearranged retreat—already occupied, no doubt by a confederate—the companion had persuaded him to leave so compromising an article of furniture. But the mulatto's heart was with it, and he was driven back to it next day, when, on reconnoitering through the window, he found policeman Walters in possession. He waited three days longer, and then his piety or his superstition drove him to try once more. Inspector Baynes, who, with his usual astuteness, had minimised the incident before me, had really recognised its importance and had left a trap into which the creature walked. Any other point, Watson?"

"The torn bird, the pail of blood, the charred bones, all the mystery of that weird kitchen?"

Holmes smiled as he turned up an entry in his note-book.

"I spent a morning in the British Museum reading up on that and other points. Here is a quotation from Eckermann's *Voodooism and the Negroid Religions*:

> 'The true voodoo-worshipper attempts nothing of importance without certain sacrifices which are intended to propitiate his unclean gods. In extreme cases these rites take the form of human sacrifices followed by cannibalism. The more usual victims are a white cock, which is plucked in pieces alive, or a black goat, whose throat is cut and body burned.'

"So you see our savage friend was very orthodox in his ritual. It is grotesque, Watson," Holmes added, as he slowly fastened his notebook, "but, as I have had occasion to remark, there is but one step from the grotesque to the horrible."